Denise

Forever

Book 1

Let's Stay Together Series

Blessings—

By:

Vanessa Miller

Vanessa
10-30-21

Forever

Vanessa Miller

Book 1
Let's Stay Together Series

Publisher's Note:

This short story is a work of fiction. References to real events, organizations, or places are used in a fictional context. Any resemblances to actual persons, living or dead are entirely coincidental.

Vanessa Miller
www.vanessamiller.com

Printed in the United States of America
© 2020 by Vanessa Miller

Praise Unlimited Enterprises
Charlotte, NC

No part of this book may be reproduced or transmitted in any form or by any means, electronic or mechanical—including photocopying, recording, or by any information storage and retrieval system—without permission in writing from the publisher.

Other Books by Vanessa Miller

Forever
Family Business I
Family Business II
Family Business III
Family Business IV
Family Business V
Family Business VI
Our Love
For Your Love
Got To Be Love
Rain in the Promised Land
Heaven Sent
Sunshine And Rain
After the Rain
How Sweet The Sound
Heirs of Rebellion
Feels Like Heaven
Heaven on Earth
The Best of All
Better for Us
Her Good Thing
Long Time Coming
A Promise of Forever Love
A Love for Tomorrow
Yesterday's Promise
Forgotten
Forgiven
Forsaken

Rain for Christmas (Novella)
Through the Storm
Rain Storm
Latter Rain
Abundant Rain
Former Rain

Anthologies (Editor)
Keeping the Faith
Have A Little Faith
This Far by Faith

Novella
Love Isn't Enough
A Mighty Love
The Blessed One (Blessed and Highly Favored series)
The Wild One (Blessed and Highly Favored Series)
The Preacher's Choice (Blessed and Highly Favored Series)
The Politician's Wife (Blessed and Highly Favored Series)
The Playboy's Redemption (Blessed and Highly Favored Series)
Tears Fall at Night (Praise Him Anyhow Series)
Joy Comes in the Morning (Praise Him Anyhow Series)
A Forever Kind of Love (Praise Him Anyhow Series)
Ramsey's Praise (Praise Him Anyhow Series)
Escape to Love (Praise Him Anyhow Series)
Praise For Christmas (Praise Him Anyhow Series)
His Love Walk (Praise Him Anyhow Series)
Could This Be Love (Praise Him Anyhow Series)
Song of Praise (Praise Him Anyhow Series)

My 50th book is dedicated to:

My wonderful, amazing husband, David Pierce. I still remember the day we met. It was many years later that we fell in love. But from now until forever, I will love and cherish you.

1

Best day ever — well, business wise anyway. Because if Jewel Dawson was truthful with herself, her best days were spent with her oh-so-so-handsome, attentive boyfriend. They'd been dating for almost two years, and every free minute Jewel had, she gladly spent it with her Baby-Boo. Well, his mama named him Jackson Lewis, but every chance Jewel got, she called him Baby-Boo.

Of course, Jackson told her not to call him that, especially when others could hear. But she had a feeling that he loved every Baby-Boo that dripped from her mouth.

Her cell rang, Jewel prayed it wasn't her client calling to cancel. But as she looked at the caller ID, she saw that it was Serena, her older sister. She put it on FaceTime before answering, so they could see each other. "Hey lady, I was going to call you later tonight."

"I wanted to get with you before you made any other plans. Kayla wants to know if we can meet at your place tomorrow to work on the party."

Kayla was their youngest sister and the organizer of the Dawson clan. That girl had once brought spreadsheets and charts to discuss a picnic the family wanted to have. "We can meet at my place, but I don't have time for Kayla turning this into some three-hour session, especially since I just might be in the mood to celebrate."

"Do tell, Sis. What are we celebrating besides mom and dad's thirty-fifth wedding anniversary?"

Flexing her shoulders, then pop and locking her arms like she was in a nineties video. Jewel was 'bout to make it do what it do. "Girl, I am parked in front of a three-million-dollar house that I'm getting ready to show to some baller. I haven't been inside yet, but from the pictures online, this place is going to sell quick."

"Jackson hooked you up with that connect?"

It was common knowledge that her Baby-Boo was a sports agent who had numerous clients in the Charlotte and Atlanta area. "He sure did. But girl, I'm nervous about this one. The highest priced home I've ever closed on was five hundred thousand. Now I'm getting ready to show this six thousand square foot monstrosity. I just hope I don't mess up."

"Pa-lease, didn't you win an award last month because of all the houses you've closed? I hate to be the one to tell you, Jewel, but you are that girl. You got this."

"Thanks for calling, Serena. You just gave me the boost of confidence I need to sell this house and two-step my way to the bank with that commission check."

"We'd all love to see you two-step again. I miss seeing you dance. You were just so graceful."

"Hush that fuss. Do you know how long ago that was? I probably can't even squeeze a thigh in those tights. But I can dance to the bank with that check." Her arms started pop locking again.

"Keep pop locking and I'm gon' ask for a loan."

A knock on her window caused Jewel's head to swivel. Here she was on FaceTime acting up with her sister instead of looking out for her client. She needed this commission. It would give her the funds she needed to pay her portion of the Antigua trip she and her sisters were planning for their parents' thirty-fifth wedding anniversary. Get yourself together, girl. Be professional and close this deal.

But as she glanced up at the person standing outside her car, all fear of losing the deal left. "Let me call you back, Serena."

She hit the end button on her cell phone and got out of the car to greet the grinning man standing next to her car. Jackson's smiles were like Christmas, hot chocolate, and a cozy fire. Wrapping her arms around him, she felt warm and safe. Just like the first time they met.

Even though neither she nor Jackson were regular churchgoers, she met him at church on Mother's Day. Jewel was there to support her mother as any dutiful daughter would. And Jackson was there to meet Aubrey Watson's parents, who just happened to be the pastor and co-pastor of the church. They bumped into each other as they were leaving the building.

Jewel glanced up at the tall, caramel toned man with midnight black eyes and dimple kissed cheeks, and she was his — he had her thinking about I-do and jumping the broom before he'd even said hello.

"What brings you here, Baby-Boo?"

"I came to see the house."

She shook her head. "You can't be here, Jackson. You know I'm showing this house to a client." Jewel looked at her watch. "He's running late, but I still don't want him to pull up and see me hanging out with my boyfriend. So unprofessional."

"Relax, Jewel, I. Am. Your. Client." He put her hand in his, "Now come on, show me this house."

Jewel pulled away as she saw her commission going, going, gone. "Did you trick me? You really don't have a friend interested in this home?"

"I *am* interested."

But Jewel wasn't having it. With hands on her hips, she demanded to know, "What are you going to do with a six thousand square foot home? I mean, I know you do a lot of entertaining, but still… no single man needs a house this big."

"What? Are you worried I won't pass the credit check?"

"This isn't funny, Jackson." She shoved him. "I was counting on this commission. You know my sisters and I are paying for our parents' trip to Antigua. I was so excited when you told me about this deal, but you were just playing games."

"Now, would your Baby-Boo do something like that to you?"

He displayed that dimpled smile that sent shivers up her spine. Jewel couldn't stay mad at this man. He had her wrapped around his finger, and he knew it. That was the sad part. She had never played hard to get with Jackson. "Come on, let me show you this house. And you better like it." They started walking toward the front door.

"I can tell you this, I already like what they did with the outside. The shrubs and flowers are nice, but this circle driveway is my jam. I've always wanted a driveway where cars could pull in and out like a drive thru. No backing up necessary."

"Then this is the perfect house for you. We don't even need to tour this place, why don't you just tell me how much you want to offer, and I'll call the owners right now."

"Jewel, play nice," he admonished.

What were they doing? Why were they even here? She shook her head, this made no sense, but if Jackson was determined to see this house, then she was going to show it to him and treat him as she would any of her other clients.

She headed down the circular driveway with Jackson. She was getting her mindset back in sell mode, but then she got an up-close look at the front of the house, the mahogany double doors, and the tan stucco with rock overlay. Her stomach turned, did flips like Simone Biles was doing her Olympic winning flips in there.

"What's wrong?"

"I don't know. My stomach feels strange." Shaking it off, she took the key out of the lockbox and opened the double doors. As they stood in the foyer, Jewel couldn't stop her mouth from opening, then closing, then opening again. Act like you been there before, girl. This is business.

Turning to Jackson, her eyes lit up. "Do you see this spiral staircase. Oh my God, this place is amazing." Dial it back a notch. She calmed it down and continued. "With this open floor plan, you can see everything from the entryway."

"What's the square footage?" Jackson asked.

Jewel opened the notes on her cell phone to get the information. "Six thousand, four hundred with five bedrooms and six bathrooms."

"Sounds perfect. And it looks like something out of the movies." Jackson pointed at the floating spiral staircase and the catwalk that spanned and overlooked the living room, dining room, and kitchen. "This joint is one hundred."

"It is very beautiful," Jewel agreed. "But don't you think it's too big for you. I mean, you travel all the time. What are you going to do with a house that has a simulation golf room, an exercise room, and a theatre room?"

"Sick." Jackson put a fist to his mouth as he tried to quench his excitement. "I didn't know this joint had simulation golf. You got to show me that."

Jewel didn't know if Jackson was just wasting her time or not. None of this was making much sense to her. Yes, she was sure he had the money to purchase this three million dollar showroom home. She just didn't understand why he wanted to. Traveling from

Charlotte to Atlanta on a regular basis kept him so busy that he hadn't even hung any paintings in his condo until Jewel bought him a few on his birthday. Did he realize how much time it would take to furnish a home this huge? But she started to loosen up, because who knows when she'd ever get to show such a grand house again. She was going to enjoy the moment. "Come on, let's find that simulation golf room together." She took Jackson's hand as they began walking through the home, searching out each room and oohing and aahing as they walked through the place.

When they made their way back to the kitchen and Jewel pointed out the cabinets and the marble countertops, Jackson leaned against the island, his eyes studied Jewel. "You love this place, don't you?"

Jewel would never buy a house like this for herself. In truth, she thought owners of monstrosities like this were just trying to show off so they could look down on the rest of the world and say, 'Look at me. I made it. Why can't you?'

But she'd never hurt Jackson's feelings like that. So she put her business girl face on. "If you like it, then Baby-Boo, I love it? It's just so big." Jewel swirled around, focusing her eyes on the kitchen. "Tell you the truth, I've never been inside a home this grand." She turned back to Jackson, looking to get his estimation of the home.

Jackson was no longer leaning against the counter. He was now on one knee with an open ring case in his hand. Jewel gasped as her eyes widened. "What are you doing?"

"Jewel Dawson, I think I fell in love with you ten minutes after we met."

"What took you so long?" Her hand was still on her chest, and she was panting but couldn't help throwing the jab, especially since she knew he was hers in one second flat.

"I'm slow, I guess." Grinning, he continued. "But I finally realized that I want to spend my life with you. What do you say we create a family in this house?"

Confusion crossed her eyes, but she was catching on fast. "You want me to move into this house with you?"

"I want you to marry me, have a couple of babies, and create a life with me." He took the ring out of the case and lifted it towards Jewel, then said, "Don't let my hand fall off. Will you please marry me?"

Her mind had traveled somewhere else when he lovingly talked about the babies and the marriage. She pulled herself back. "Of course, I will. Oh, my God. I had no idea." She stretched out her hand so he could put the diamond ring on her finger.

Jackson stood, he pulled her into an embrace and then kissed her with an abandon that she'd never felt from him before. "Baby, you have just made me the happiest man alive."

"I'm happy too, Jackson. I had hoped that you and I would one day get married, but I had no idea that you were ready for such a commitment."

"You and me against the world, baby. That's how you and your Baby-Boo are doing life from now on."

Jewel liked the sound of that. Her great grandparents had been married for seventy-five years before they died within two days of each other. Her grandparents have now been married for fifty-seven years, and her parents are getting ready to celebrate thirty-five years of marriage. Jewel didn't take it lightly that she was getting ready to join them in a most sacred union.

Jackson's family didn't share the same values about marriage as her family did, but they would be okay. They had to be because when anyone in the Dawson family said I-do, it was truly until death and all that. Selah.

2

All day long, Jewel couldn't stop smiling. She kept looking at her engagement ring, which was a three-carat, square-cut diamond, platinum band with diamond studs wrapped around it. The ring was exquisite, Jewel couldn't have loved it more even if she had picked it out herself. But in truth, Jackson could have given her a less expensive ring, and she still would have loved it, because of the love she had for her man.

"It just ain't right, my younger sister will make it down the aisle before I do," Serena teased.

"It'll happen for you, Serena. After all, if you hadn't stayed with Drake so long, you probably would have already found the one and married him by now."

"Don't put me into depression thinking about that seven-year mistake. It's hard enough knowing that mom is going to be pitying me, so please don't have a long engagement. Just rush that man down the aisle and get it over and done with already."

Jewel pulled into the parking lot and turned off her car. "I don't like the way you sound. Do I need to ask Kayla to be my maid-of-honor or what?"

"I wish you would ask Kayla. You know I would love to be your maid-of-honor. I'm just messing with you. Because in truth, I am over the moon happy for you. My sister is not just getting married, but her man is buying her a three-million-dollar home."

"And that big sis is the only problem I have."

"What problem… I don't see no problem."

"I'm serious, Serena. Jackson was so excited about buying that house for us. I just don't know how to tell him that I don't want it. Something about that house turned my stomach. When has a house ever done that to me? I sell houses for a living. And love looking at them. But I hated this house before I even walked inside. Don't get me wrong, it's beautiful but way too expensive."

"Girl, your man has money. Let him spoil you."

Jewel shook her head as if her sister could see through the phone. "I don't care about his money. What if he lost all of his clients and had to get a regular job? Do you think we'd be able to afford that big house then? Not on my salary. I just think we need to be a little more sensible."

"Out of the three Dawson sisters, you have always been the more sensible one. Because I would have just said, 'yes and thank you'."

Glancing at the time, Jewel opened her car door. "Let me get in here. My last clients were not impressed with the house I just showed them. They have four hundred thousand to spend, so I need to drum up some more properties with the quickness."

"Don't forget that we're meeting at your place tonight to finalize our plans for the anniversary party," Serena reminded her as they hung up.

Heading into her office, reading the sign above that said, Mercer Realty, Jewel reminded herself of the other reason she didn't want to invest in such an expensive property so early in their marriage. Her future plans included owning her own realty company. That took money, and she had been saving every spare penny for the last two years.

She had to make Jackson understand that she didn't want to be totally dependent on his income. She wanted to be able to truly be a help to him if needed. And with her future goals in mind, she didn't feel like she could be helpful and still meet her goals if they purchased that house.

She was thinking about making her man a nice meal as she stepped into the building. Jackson loved Ribeye steak. He especially loved the way she cooked it. So, she would pick up some steaks and invite him over for dinner and tell him how she really felt.

Passing the front desk, Jewel noticed a huge bouquet of red, pink, and white roses. Patty, the receptionist, once told her that her husband sends roses whenever he's in the doghouse. Jewel wondered what Patty's man had done to her this time. She was just about to get in Patty's business, but the receptionist jumped out of her seat the moment she saw Jewel and picked up the vase.

"Look who's getting roses at work now," Patty said. "I hope that boyfriend of yours hasn't gotten himself in the doghouse." She tsk-tsked as she handed Jewel the vase. "Thirty-six roses, he must be in big trouble."

Jewel lifted her hand and showed off her ring finger. "He's not in trouble at all. Just in love with his lady." Jewel didn't like bragging like that, but how dare Patty assume that her husband was anything like her Baby-Boo.

Inhaling her beautiful roses, Jewel smiled as she set the flowers on her desk. She truly loved Jackson and was so happy they were going to spend a lifetime together. She turned on her computer and began searching for properties suitable for her clients' four hundred thousand dollar budget, all the while dreaming of how wonderful life would be when she and Jackson found their dream home.

Jewel had just spotted a five-bedroom, with a home office and an extra space that could be used for a game room or movie room when there came a knock on her door. This house was perfect for her clients, so she jotted down the info as she said, "Come in."

Patty stepped in, carrying a legal-sized white envelope. "Hey, I forgot to hand this to you. It was delivered with the roses."

A puzzled look crossed Jewel's eyes. She had received small envelopes or Valentine's Day cards with flowers, but never an envelope long enough for a letter. Had Jackson written her a poem? She wouldn't put it past him. Her Baby-Boo could be so romantic when he put his mind to it. "Thank you, Patty."

Jewel took the envelope, as Patty walked out of her office, she opened it, excited about what she would find. After all, a man that sends you not just one, not two, but three dozen roses had to be very creative. But the paper that slid out of the envelope wasn't poetic at all. It was a document that broke Jewel's heart as she read each and every word.

Jackson Lewis and Jewel Dawson, who shall collectively be known as "the party", truly love each other and are entering into this prenuptial agreement in contemplation of marriage.

The party due hereby agree that their rights for ownership and division of all property belonging to either of the party before marriage and all property that may be acquired by either or both of them after marriage shall stay with its respective owner. This agreement shall also set forth spousal support or maintenance as required.

In consideration of the fact that unhappy differences may arise between the party, the party desire that the terms set forth in this agreement will govern the distribution of their present and future property and/or assets, to as great a degree as permitted by statutory or case law. Furthermore, the party intend that any federal or state legislation which may be applicable shall not be applied to them.

Stunned, shocked, and sizzling with anger boiling inside. Jewel was about to explode like a teapot whistling its warning. Grabbing her handbag, Jewel stuffed the prenup inside, and stormed out of her office.

"Hey, where are you going?" Patty stood with the phone in her hand as Jewel raced past her. "Mr. Cotton is on the phone. He and his wife found another house they want to see."

"Send him to my voicemail and tell him I'll give him a call back." Jewel didn't give Patty an explanation. She didn't have time to even concern herself with how the woman felt about Jewel not handling her business at work, cause she had some other business to handle.

Never in life had she ever imagined that she would marry a man who was thinking about an exit strategy before they even began planning the wedding. What kind of man was she marrying? Did he really think that she was only interested in getting her hands on his money?

Jewel saw red as she drove straight to Jackson's office. How dare he do something like this. Did he really have such a low opinion of her? Did he think that she was so money hungry that she would marry a man just to turn around and divorce him so she could get the gold?

Jewel stomped right up to the reception desk, didn't bother to greet the woman as she usually did. Pointing to Jackson's office door, she asked, "Is he in?"

The receptionist hit the hold button and moved the phone receiver from her ear. "He's on a phone conference right now. But if you have a seat, I'll let him know that you're here."

Jewel ignored the request. Walking past the receptionist's desk, she shoved open the double doors to Jackson's office and stormed in.

Jackson glanced up and smiled as he removed the phone from his ear. He lifted a finger. "Give me one moment, bae."

The receptionist ran into the office, behind Jewel and tried to urge her out. Jewel wasn't having any of it. She slammed the prenup on Jackson's desk. "How dare you!"

Speaking into the phone, Jackson said, "Uh, Matt, I need to call you back." Rising from his chair as he hung the phone up. "Do you know who that was?"

"No, and don't care."

Jackson jabbed a finger toward the phone that he just hung up. "That was Matt Rhule, the coach for the Panthers. I've been trying to get a meeting with him for weeks to discuss Scottie's new contract."

Jewel knew who Scottie was. Jackson had been representing the twenty-year-old since he went to the Panthers in the fourth round of the 2018 draft. With Cam Newton going down from injuries, Scottie and McCaffrey had been two bright spots. McCaffrey had already received his extension, now Jackson wanted to make sure that the Panthers understood that Scottie also needed an upgrade. But Jewel didn't care about any of that right now.

"What kind of man would send some mess like this the day after proposing to the woman he wants to marry."

An eyebrow lifted, lines appeared on his forehead. "I don't get what you're so upset about."

Eyes popping, hands flaring. "You're kidding, right? You send me flowers and a prenup, and you don't know why I'm upset."

"Did you like the flowers? I thought they would make your day since you like flowers so much."

That gleam in his eyes did something to Jewel. Made her think about their third date when he looked at her like he'd found what he'd spent a lifetime searching for. From that moment, she had felt safe with him. But no more. "I don't think I ever want flowers from you again. You have completely spoiled it for me with this prenup business."

"What is so wrong with a prenup? In the circles I run in, it's viewed as marital suicide to get married without one."

"Then, you're running in the wrong circles."

He walked towards her and put a hand on her arm. "Look, Bae, I'm not trying to insult you or anything. But it's not wise for us to get married without the prenup."

"Why? Do you really think I'm after your money? And that I'm just going to divorce you as soon as the going gets tough?"

"I've seen it happen to too many men in the sports field. I'm just a sports agent, but I've managed to make a pretty good living, and I can't just let you or anyone else walk away with half my stuff. But that prenup is very generous. If you let your attorney look over it, I'm sure he'll advise you to sign it."

Jewel backed away from him. She couldn't believe that this was the man she had fallen in love with. "You're actually planning our divorce before our marriage."

"That's absurd, Jewel. Why would I want to divorce you? I just asked to marry you."

Shaking her head, she closed her eyes, trying to stop the tears, but they came anyway. Her eyes refocused on Jackson as tears drifted down her face. "My parents have been married for thirty-five years. My grandparents just celebrated fifty-seven years of marriage, and my great grandparents died a few days after each other after spending most of their lives together."

"That's great, Bae. But you've got to understand where I'm coming from because my dad is on his fourth marriage… I just don't have good examples like you."

"Maybe your dad just chose the wrong women. But I won't choose the wrong man, Jackson. I won't love you and plan a life with you just to have you one day treat me like I'm nothing. Throw me out and go on with your life like there never was a Jewel and Jackson."

"But it's not like that, Jewel. I just need to know that you're in this for the right reason. And signing that prenup will give me a level of comfort."

Jewel touched her ring finger. Her engagement ring hadn't even been on her finger a full twenty-four hours. She hadn't even gotten used to wearing it yet. And now she was taking it off and handing it back to Jackson. "I didn't fall for you because of your money. I didn't even know you had money until our fifth date, and by then, I was already on Team Jackson. I just didn't know you didn't believe that our love could last."

Jackson refused to reach out and take the ring. "You're talking about a fairytale, Jewel. Marriage has about a fifty-fifty chance these days. Less than that with celebrities."

"You're not a celebrity, Jackson. You just represent them. And dummy me, thought you knew the difference." She put the ring on his desk and headed for the door, wiping the tears from her face.

He reached out and grabbed her. "Don't Jewel. Don't do this. You and I belong together. There will always be a Jewel and Jackson if I have anything to say about it. Don't let a little thing like a prenup come between us."

Shaking her head, she told him, "You just don't get it." She pried his hand off her arm, walked out of his office and away from his kind of love.

3

At home in her condo, crying like she had a death sentence, and the jailer had just asked her to pick her last meal. Jewel's eyes were bloodshot and puffy when the doorbell rang. She went to the door to peek out, already fixing her mind for how she was going to get Jackson told if he had the nerve to be standing on the other side of that door.

But it wasn't Jackson. "Oh, no." Jewel put a hand over her mouth and contemplated ignoring them. She'd forgotten that her sisters were coming over tonight.

"What are you doing? Open the door already," Serena said.

"I'm not in the mood for company. Can we do this tomorrow?" Jewel put the tissue she'd been holding up to her nose and blew.

"Open this door and let us in. You know we have to get everything finalized for mom and dad's thirty-fifth celebration, or there will be no trip, and no vow renewal next month."

Being the oldest, Serena was also the bossiest. It burned Jewel that Serena could tell everybody what to do and when to do it. But this time, she was spot on. They had to finalize the details for the big anniversary bash they were planning for their parents. She would just have to put a hold on her breakdown and let her sisters in. She unlocked the door, then went into the kitchen to throw her disgusting snot rag away. As she was washing her hands, her sisters enter the kitchen.

"Oh my God, what happened to you?" Kayla dropped the notebooks and her laptop bag at the kitchen table and rushed over to Jewel.

"I'm good. Don't worry about me." She splashed some water on her face and sat down at the table. She turned to Serena. "Can I borrow some paper and a pen so I can keep up with Kayla's number crunching?"

Serena's lip twisted as her head went no, no, no. "Uh-uh, wait one minute. You think you gon' be looking like Scary Carrie up in here and we ain't gon' ask no questions." She shook her head again. "It don't work like that, so spill it already."

"Yeah," Kayla agreed. "Who did what, and how bad do you want us to hurt him?"

Serena might be the bossy one, but Kayla was always ready for a fight. And the crazy thing about it was Kayla was the shortest one of the three of them. Jewel and Serena both looked like their father and took their height from him. But Kayla was Vanetta Dawson's daughter through and through. Looks, height, attitude. As far as Jewel was concerned, all the Dawson girls were pretty, but Kayla was on another level. She just didn't know it, and with the way she always wore her hair in a ponytail with little to no make-up, it was hard for anyone to truly see her beauty. "You need to be worrying about getting a relaxer and doing something with all that hair on that gorgeous head of yours, rather than looking for a fight."

Kayla put a hand to her head. "Forget about some relaxer. I am natural and proud of it. You just wait, keep letting that hairdresser straighten your hair… one morning, chunks of it will be on your pillow."

"Don't let our sister change the subject, Kayla." Serena took Jewel's left hand and ran her hand over it. "What happened to that beautiful engagement ring you told me about? Talk to us. You don't have to go through this alone."

Even if her eyes hadn't been bloodshot and puffy, Jewel doubted she would have been able to hide the unbearable pain she was feeling from Serena. Because her sister knew what it felt like to love and lose. Jewel thought she was all cried out, but fresh tears escaped and trickled down her face again. "He doesn't want to get married. Not for real, for real."

"Oooh, I'ma call Mama." Kayla took her cell out.

Jewel took the cell phone from her go-tell-it-on-the-mountain sister. "I don't want her in my business. Why you always running our business back to Mama?"

"She is the Dawson family spy," Serena agreed. "But Mama might be able to talk some sense into Jackson."

"I mean, he did take Mama to the jewelry store to pick out your engagement ring. So, I think he might listen to her."

Jewel felt like Oprah Winfrey in the Color Purple when she'd said, 'I don't know y'all no more' as she looked at Kayla. Surely, she must have heard her baby sister wrong. "Y'all knew Jackson was going to propose to me last night?"

Kayla held up a hand. "Calm down, Sis. I didn't know when he was going to ask. I only knew that he had the ring."

"I knew. He told me all about the house," Serena admitted.

"Faker." Jewel pointed an accusing finger at Serena. "You sat on that phone with me, listening as I bragged about selling a three-million-dollar house when all the while you knew Jackson was the client." Before Serena could respond, Jewel added, "And why didn't you tell him that I have no use for such a big house like that? Y'all

all up in my business, why can't y'all be good little snitches and spies?"

"Girl, bye." Serena waved a dismissive hand. "If a man wants to buy you a mansion, you shut up and take it."

"It's too big for my taste." Jewel shook her head. "Just think, last night I thought an oversized house was the only problem I had to tackle, now I'm sitting here crying like a fool."

"If you don't open your mouth and tell us what happened, we are going to start thinking that you are some kind of fool. Because we know for a fact that Jackson wants to marry you."

Jewel wiped her face. "Okay, Kayla, you're right. Jackson does want to marry me, he just doesn't want to do what it takes to stay married. He had a prenup sent to my job today, and I just couldn't believe he would do something like that."

Serena leaned back in her seat. Sucked her teeth. "He never mentioned anything about that."

"I've got a headache." Jewel went into the bathroom, popped two pain pills, and came back to the kitchen. "Can we look over the anniversary plans. I don't want to talk about Jackson tonight. It's just too raw, too real right now."

Serena nodded and turned to Kayla. "Has dad confirmed his vacation time?"

"Wait a minute." Jewel was about to spaz out. "I thought mom had dad put in vacation for their anniversary months ago."

"She did. But another manager put in for the same week, so he wasn't sure he was going to get it. The company needs at least one of them to oversee the accounting department."

"Kayla, why didn't you tell me this before I paid the deposit for the ballroom?"

Serena held up a hand to halt the impending argument between her sisters. "This is actually a good thing. Mom and Dad normally go to Myrtle Beach for their anniversary. But since he had this issue, they never confirmed their yearly reservation."

Jewel didn't know if she was bugging because things in her life had blown up, or if she generally had reason to be concerned. "I still don't see how this helps us. Since we are paying for mom, dad's, Grandma Priscilla and Pop-Pop's rooms for the five days and the ballroom which is totally close to fifteen thousand, we'd better make sure that dad can get away, or we'll all be at that island resort looking at each other; and I'll be mad about the money we spent."

Flipping through a few pages in her notebook, Kayla showed the girls a few papers. "Actually, we won't be out of much money because we don't have to pay for the hotel rooms until we arrive. And all we've paid so far is the two thousand dollar deposit."

"You mean, all I've paid because the two of you haven't given me one dime on that deposit. But I'm not sweating it. Because I know we're splitting this three ways. And I have faith that y'all good job having sisters will come through."

"We got you," Serena told her.

"And I'm working on getting my money together." Kayla smiled sweetly at her sisters. "But y'all know I just started my event planning business, and I could really use some more clients."

Jewel meant what she said. She trusted her sisters. They wouldn't leave her holding the bag. She just hoped her dad would come through with those vacation days. But Jewel knew better than anybody that men just didn't do what you wanted them to do when you needed them to do it.

~~~

Jackson had the ball. Dribble, dribble. Then as he reached mid-court, standing smack dab in the center circle, he released the ball. All the guys on the court heads followed from release to the swish of the ball as it went straight through the hoop. The game halted as even the guys on the opposing team dapped him up.

"Okay, Steph Curry, I see you." John, his frat brother and longtime friend, gave him some dap. "You missed your calling. You should've been playing on the court instead of making deals for knuckleheads that don't appreciate how hard you work."

John and Jackson had spent two years hoopin' at UNC. Then John got drafted after his sophomore year. Jackson stayed at UNC and graduated without having any prospect of being drafted. So, he appreciated John for saying that. But he also knew that he was much better suited as an agent rather than a baller. And Jackson was okay with that.

"I'm not a knucklehead, Mr. Lewis. I appreciate everything you're doing for me and my family."

Jackson's smile dropped as he heard his young client call him Mr. Lewis. Aubrey Watson's family sacrificed everything for his hoop dreams. Aubrey was a star, and his light was about to shine just as big as some of the top dogs like LeBron and Steph. He just had to get the boy to believe in himself. Stop kowtowing like he owed everybody something. "Don't call me Mr. ever again. Soon we'll all be calling you Mister. You hear me?"

Aubrey was holding the basketball to his chest like if he let it go, all his hoop dreams would go with it. "Yeah, I hear you. But my Mama don't play that. She taught me to respect my elders."

At 6'2, Jackson couldn't reach 6'9 Aubrey's head so he could muff it. So, he snatched the basketball from him and playfully popped him in the chest with it. "This elder just spanked you and your teammates in some b-ball, so I'm not as old as you think, huh?"

"You're in your thirties, Mr. — I mean, Jackson." Aubrey shrugged like that said it all.

John looked the boy over. Smirked. "For a nineteen-year-old, I guess we do look like a couple of old guys to you. But we still got lessons to teach. So, watch yourself."

Aubrey gave John some dap. "Thanks for the business lessons today. And I will keep my eyes open."

Jackson walked out with Aubrey. When the young man got to his car, Jackson opened the door for him. "The information I'm getting is that you are top five in the draft, Mr. Watson. So, get ready for this ride. And don't you ever think anyone has done you a favor. You've earned everything that's coming to you."

As Aubrey got in his beat down old Chevy, he pointed heavenward. "I owe everything to God. He's been good to me. He's the one I don't ever want to forget. Because all the fame and fortune can come and go, but without God, I would miss the mark every time."

Jackson stood in the parking lot watching Aubrey drive off as he wondered if he had misunderstood who this young man was the entire time. He'd spotted Aubrey during his junior year in high school. Wined and dined his parents for a year straight, offered suggestions on which college would be best for Aubrey's talents to shine. When Aubrey didn't take his suggestion to sign with Duke, he thought he and the young rising star were parting ways. But the family reached out to him. They said it was important to them that Aubrey attend his father's alma mater.

They chose Auburn University. And even though Virginia beat them in the 2019 NCAA championship game, Aubrey's star rose to new heights. It wasn't one of the Virginia boys slated for one of the top five picks, it was his client. But Jackson hadn't realized how serious his client was about the Lord at that time.

He probably should've had a clue since his parents were pastors. But now he saw Aubrey in a whole new light. The young man wasn't kowtowing to people because of his family. He was trying to be respectful because of his own relationship with the Lord.

Jackson wasn't religious, but he had mad respect for the kid. That changed everything about the strategy he was going to use when accepting endorsements for the kid. Aubrey could make fists full of money and still keep his integrity. Jackson would make sure of that.

Back in the gym, he sat down in the bleachers with John. "Thanks for helping out with Aubrey today. He is a good kid."

"I get that impression." John clasped his hands together and looked directly at his friend. "But what was up with you today?"

"Oh, you mad 'cause I took the winning shot? When you gon' let stuff like that go. Back in college, it was the same ole stuff. Always had to take the big shots."

"That's because I was the star of the team, and the coach demanded that I take those big shots."

Jackson couldn't even get his back up about John saying he was the star on the team because it was true. He'd even made the All-Star team twice while in the NBA. But after eight years, his career was cut short due to a back injury that made him go sit down somewhere. Now he had a gig with ESPN and was able to talk basketball and critique other players.

"But I'm not mad about you taking your shot today. But some of the elbows wasn't necessary. I'm not trying to get injured in a pick-up game."

Jackson bumped his fist to his chest a couple of times. "Bro, sorry 'bout that. I didn't realize I was going that hard."

"Well, is it work, or is it the little woman?"

Jackson wanted to act like he didn't know what John was getting at. But it wasn't even worth it. He played angry because he was angry. "Man, Jewel flipped on me." He scratched his head. "And I don't know what to do about it."

"I thought things were going real good. Didn't you just order a ring for her?"

"Gave it to her. Even let her tour the house I want to buy for us… the whole bit."

"Don't tell me she said no. That don't seem like Jewel. I've seen y'all together, that girl loves you."

"Yeah, it's all love, until the light bill comes due."

"Tell me about it. But at least we got the cash to pay the bills." John and Jackson high-fived.

"But the thing I don't get is how a woman can claim she don't want your money, but in the next breath, tell you she's not signing no prenup." His forehead lines appeared again. "What's that about?"

"You gotta have that prenup. We all know how it goes. One minute these women love you and can't live without you. The next minute they're embarrassed because you got caught on TMZ with some fill-in chick."

Jackson was trying not to laugh because John really did break up with his first wife over a cheating scandal that had been caught on TMZ. Why he ever expected her to stay while he made a fool out of her on national television was something Jackson couldn't comprehend. Cheating was out of the question. He'd watched his father lose three marriages because of his active sex life outside of the home. Jackson had waited until thirty-five to even think about marriage because he wanted to make sure that he was ready for that kind of commitment. John should have done the same. "Yo, you earned that divorce, bro."

John nodded. "True that. But what one won't put up with, another one will. I'm just trying to make the best of this second marriage."

"Is everything good?"

John shrugged. "I miss my kids. It just ain't the same. Marissa acts like I'm trying to steal them away from her when I have them at the house."

"So, you think I need to let the whole prenup thing go?"

John looked at Jackson as if he'd lost his whole mind. "Are you a fool? I might miss my kids, but at least I'm not missing my dollars."

4

Vanetta Dawson was busy moving from one side of the kitchen to the other while Jewel, Serena, and Kayla stood around the kitchen island, helping where needed. Serena chopped veggies, Kayla made the cornbread. Jewel worked her fork, smashing her mother's famous smashed potatoes with chipotle gouda cheese, green onions, and sour cream. The flavorful cheese made the potatoes taste like bacon had been added to the mixture. If Jewel became half the cook her mother was, her future husband would stick and stay just so he could have a good meal on Sundays. Jewel was real with it. She was too busy to be in the kitchen every day of the week.

She no longer had that to worry about. But Jewel wasn't ready to give her mother that information just yet. Vanetta hadn't liked Serena's I-wanna-live-with-you-but-not-marry-you man who had loitered in her life for seven years too long. But when Serena broke up with him, their mother moped around the house for a whole week. She'd even cried as she had lamented about being the only one of her friends who hadn't planned a wedding for a daughter or held a grandchild in her arms.

So, no way did Jewel want to tell her that another Dawson girl had gotten into a relationship that wouldn't lead to marriage and a baby. Jewel just kept smashing those potatoes and praying that her mother wouldn't notice her ring-less finger. Jewel didn't even want her drama queen of a mother to ask any questions about her less than twenty-four-hour engagement. Please don't ask. Please don't ask.

But on cue, Vanetta turned to Jewel. Her eyes squinted, "You're not wearing your charm bracelet."

Glancing down at her wrist, Jewel's eyes widened. If her mother noticed her wrist, she would soon ask why she wasn't wearing her engagement ring. The woman helped Jackson pick it out, she would know that he'd already given it to her. She put her hands deeper into the bowl as if she was going to kneed the potatoes rather than fork them. "I must have left it at home."

"Just strange seeing you without it."

Jewel knew why her mother felt that way. Vanetta had given Jewel the bracelet when she was sixteen with a cross hanging from it and a ballerina. Then when she turned eighteen, her mother gave her an open faced-Bible charm and told her to always remember who God created her to be. Her mother had purchased each of her girls a charm bracelet. Jewel tried to live up to it, but once she went off to college, she took the ballerina off and replaced it with a shoe. Jewel loved shoes.

"You are mashing them potatoes like they did something to you," Vanetta teased her. "Have you made this dish for Jackson?"

Of course, she'd let Jackson sample the Dawson family smashed potatoes. She'd fixed a few other things her mother had taught them as well. But this was not the day to talk about that. "Mom, you already asked me that, remember?"

Serena chimed in. "Yeah, Mama. I remember Jewel telling you how much Jackson loved the potatoes. Next question. You haven't grilled Kayla lately. And I think she had a date last week."

Vanetta pursed her lips as she gave her oldest a disapproving look. "I don't grill you girls." But then she turned to Kayla. "Who'd you go out with? How come you didn't tell me about him?"

Kayla picked up one of the onions she had been chopping and threw it at Serena. "It was just lunch. Nothing special, and I haven't heard from him since."

This was the first time Jewel was hearing this. She felt like a bad sister for not asking Kayla about her date. "Ah, Kayla. You should have told me. I know you had high hopes for that guy."

"Not a biggie. The one who is for me will recognize my value. Right Mama?"

Jewel smiled at her sister; she was such a brown noser.

"I'm glad you've been listening to me. Of course, he will recognize your value. I'm so glad my girls know their worth." Vanetta took the meatloaf out of the oven just as the doorbell rang. She turned to Jewel. "Can you get the door?"

Why me? She wanted to ask just as the three of them used to do when they were teenagers, and their mother asked either of them to do anything. They always wanted to know why she didn't ask one of the other girls like they were being punished or something. But she was too old for that kind of pettiness. She wiped her hands and headed for the front door, mumbling under her breath about how one of her sisters was going to get the door the next time. "Who is it?"

Jewel asked the question but didn't wait for the answer as she flung the door open and then found herself standing in front of Mr. Love-em-and-ask-em-to-sign-a-prenup himself. She put a hand on his chest and shoved him backward. Closing the door, they stood on the porch. "What are you doing here?"

"What?" He shrugged. "Your mom called and invited me to Sunday brunch. At least she is one Dawson woman that knows how to treat a man."

Folding her arms across her chest, she rolled her eyes. "How do you know it's not my father who knows how to keep a wife happy? Some men know how to do that."

"I'm sure there are," Jackson agreed. "Maybe I'll ask him for a few lessons. Sure can't get 'em from my dad."

The front door cracked open, Kayla peeked her head out. "Mom wants to know why you are out here on the porch."

Jewel turned toward her sister. "Tell her I'm on my way."

"With Jackson, right? She knows Jackson is out here with you."

"Please close the door, Kayla." Taking a deep breath, Jewel turned back to Jackson. She loved her mother dearly, just wished she wasn't such a busybody when it came to her children's love lives.

Jackson moved past Jewel and put his hand on the doorknob. "Where do you think you're going?"

"Mama Dawson wants us in the house. The food is probably ready, and I'm hungry."

Jewel shook her head. "Oh no you don't. I am not comfortable with you being here. You and I aren't on good terms."

"But have you told your mother that?"

Jewel didn't answer.

"I didn't think so." The look on Jackson's face was smug. "I can go in and tell her that we've called off the engagement. Maybe you'll have a better dinner with the family then, huh?" Hand on the doorknob, he inched open the door.

Jewel jumped in front of him and closed the door back. There was no way that she was about to sit through dinner with the disappointing look that would be on her mother's face once Jackson told her there wasn't going to be a wedding. "I'm not prepared for this. I can't with my mother right now."

"No worries, my lady," he said like an English gent as he bowed low and then reached into his jacket pocket and pulled out the ring she'd left on his desk. "I came prepared."

She shook her head. Backed away like he'd pulled anthrax out of his pocket and was about to throw it on her.

"Look, you don't want your mother to know that we called off the engagement, right?"

"Right."

"Don't you think she'll be suspicious if you're not wearing the ring that she just knew you'd love?"

Her mother thought she knew her so well. But Jewel had to admit that she loved everything about that princess cut diamond ring. She had wanted to wear it forever. No use fighting it, he was right. She stretched out her hand. He put the ring back on her finger. "I'll get it back to you just as soon as I tell my mom the truth. I just don't want to spoil her happiness with all our plans for her and daddy's anniversary celebration."

"Still Antigua?"

Smiling as Jewel thought about how much her parents would love their surprise, she nodded. "That's why I don't want to ruin this for them. My parents worked hard, putting us three girls through college. They sacrificed a lot. Now the house is paid off, Dad is about to retire, and they've finally saved enough to enjoy life. We want to treat them to something they wouldn't have paid for themselves."

"I get that, and you're a good daughter to think of your mother's feelings."

Jewel wasn't only thinking of her mother's feelings. She also wanted her dad to be able to enjoy the vacation get-a-way they had planned. And if Vanetta Dawson moped around Antigua for the whole five days of their celebration — Daddy didn't deserve that. "Okay, come have dinner with us. We'll tell the family about our break-up once we return from the trip."

Jackson nodded. "Now, I need you to do something for me."

"What? Boy bye. You and your selfishness are the problem. You don't get to ask for favors."

"Okay, have it your way. I'll just go let Mama Dawson know that I can't stay for dinner because you don't want to marry me anymore."

Squinting her eyes at him, she said, "See what I mean about your selfishness. You don't even care that you're going to ruin my mom and dad's thirty-fifth-anniversary celebration."

"All I want is dinner."

"What?" Sometimes Jackson threw curve balls that Jewel just couldn't catch. "Aren't we getting ready to have dinner." She pointed at the house. "In there."

"Yeah, but that's with your family. I'm having dinner tomorrow night with my dad and his new wife. I want you there. And then when we're done with dinner, I want you to tell me why you are so opposed to prenups." He lifted his hands. "That's it. That's all I'm asking for. You get a free meal, you get to meet my new stepmom, and you get to tell me how awful you think I am."

"Your dad is very charming, unlike his son." She playfully shoved Jackson's shoulder. "I guess it's the least I can do."

Jackson popped his shoulders as he rubbed his stomach. "All right then. Let's eat."

"I was beginning to think I'd have to come out there and pull the two of you in here by your ears." Vanetta frowned as they entered the dining room. "Your daddy don't like to wait on his dinner. You know that."

Jewel sat down at the table. "Yes, Mama, I know that." She glanced at her father, sitting at the head of the table, and smiled. "Sorry, Daddy."

Jackson sat down next to Bradley Dawson. "Thanks for the invite to dinner."

Vanetta said, "You're welcome."

A small salad had been placed on the table in front of every chair. The meatloaf, smash potatoes, green beans, and diner rolls were in the middle of the table. Bradley asked everyone to, "Bow your heads."

They did so. "Lord, we thank you for this food, let it be nourishment for our bodies. Cast out any impurities, because they are not worthy of children of God. In Jesus name we pray, Amen."

Bradley then picked up the meatloaf, took a piece, then passed the tray to Jackson. The others began filling their dinner plates with the assortment and passing trays around so everyone could fill their plates.

"This smells so good, Mrs. Vanetta. And you already know how much I love those smashed red potatoes."

"Boy, I told you to call me Mama, or Mama Dawson."

"Of course, Mama Dawson. I just wasn't sure if Jewel was ready to hear me plant myself so firmly in the family like that."

Jewel side-eyed him for trying to start trouble. She would have kicked him under the table if he had been sitting next to her.

Vanetta harrumphed. "Far as I'm concerned, you're the son I didn't haven't to get one stretch mark for and didn't have to throw up not one time. So, you are family."

Bradley took a few bites of his meatloaf and then turned his attention to Jewel. "That's a mighty fine ring you're wearing today. Something you want to tell us?"

Jewel hesitated. She looked at the ring that had meant so much to her a few days ago. But now, she just saw it as a symbol of lies. Her parents didn't raise her to be deceitful. But she had to find a way to spare them the truth for a whole two weeks.

Jackson cleared his throat. "I spoke to you last week about my intentions, Mr. Dawson."

Jewel's head popped up. Her eyes filled with adoration, even though she tried not to feel anything for Jackson. But that caramel skin tone of his went so well with his luscious lips. Lips that had just informed her that he'd spoken with her father before asking her to marry him. She'd never thought to demand that of him, but that was exactly what she would have wanted her man to do. She doubted she'd ever told Jackson her feelings on the matter. How did he know?

"Yes, you did. And I appreciated the lunch and the words you spoke." A look of mischief shined brightly on Bradley's face as he continued. "Now that you're part of the family, I suppose the missus and I can get a membership at that swanking country club you took me too, right?"

Vanetta let out a laugh as she lovingly gazed at her husband. "You've been bragging about that club for a week now. I bet it's nothing more than a hole in the wall. Just like that chicken place you like so much."

"Don't you put your mouth on the Chicken Coop. Some of the best chicken in Charlotte comes out of that so-called hole in the wall."

"Y'all hear him?" Vanetta glanced at everyone at the table. "Someone please tell your father that he is too old to be munching on fried chicken twice a week."

"Keep talking, woman, and I'll take you to the Chicken Coop for our anniversary. Even let you order the shrimp."

Laughter erupted around the table. Everyone, that is, except Vanetta, was laughing. She was actually gazing at her husband like he was a tasty piece of fried chicken. "That reminds me of that soul food restaurant you took me to for our first anniversary."

Bradley was smiling at his wife also. "We didn't have much back then, but we still managed to enjoy our anniversary, didn't we old girl?"

"The food was terrible. But that was probably one of our best anniversaries we've had so far." Vanetta glanced over at Serena and then giggled like a schoolgirl with a secret.

Serena looked around the room. "What? Why you laughing at me, Mama?"

Bradley leaned back in his seat at the head of the table, wiped his mouth after swallowing a forkful of meatloaf. Looking every bit like the king on his throne. "Your Mama's not laughing at you, girl. She's just remembering the night we conceived our first child." He looked back at his wife. "Bad food — good loving. I'll toast to that." He lifted his iced-tea glass and toasted the air.

Vanetta threw a napkin at him. "Hush up, Bradley."

"Eeewww." Serena got up from the table with her plate in hand. "I'm not listening to this." She took her plate into the kitchen and sat down at the island. The dining room was open to the kitchen, so they could see her at the kitchen island. That only caused the group to laugh even more.

Before returning his fork back to his plate, Bradley turned back to Jackson. "See why I want that country club membership? My sweet Netta loved me when all I could afford was a bad meal at a local restaurant. I've been trying to make up for that anniversary for thirty-four years now." He shook his head. "I couldn't even afford a hotel room back then. But I can afford one now… and I can pay for that fancy country club too. And I'm going to take her to that club to celebrate our anniversary."

Jackson glanced over at Jewel with questioning eyes. "But I thought…"

Jewel shook her head. Pursed her lips tight, praying that Jackson would get the message and not spoil the surprise she and her sisters had worked so hard to pull off. She heard Kayla's intake of breath. Serena got up from the kitchen counter like she was about to tackle Jackson in order to shut him up.

"What's that?" Bradley looked at Jackson, waiting on him to finish.

"Oh nothing, it just seemed like you and Mama Dawson didn't let nothing stop y'all from enjoying that first anniversary."

Bradley winked at Jackson. "One day, I'll tell you a little more about that night."

"Oh no, you won't," Jewel objected. "We don't need any more visuals about your baby-making skills. Passing on that."

Bradley glanced at his wife. "I'm not embarrassing you, am I, sweet Netta?"

"No, baby. But I keep telling you that you have nothing to make up for. I would have rather eaten at that soul food restaurant with you, bad food an all than to have tea with the Queen."

"Even after all these years," Bradley questioned. The look in his eyes said he needed that answer.

"Especially after all these years. I'm Team Dawson, all the way."

"Then let's toast to that." Bradley put his glass in the air, and the rest of the family join him. "Team Dawson!"

Vanetta shook her head at Jewel as they brought the glasses back down. "Remember what I tell you. You are not on Team Dawson anymore. You are now and forevermore, Team Lewis."

Jewel jumped backward in her seat as if someone had attempted to slap her.

Jackson stood. Lifted his glass toward her. "Team Lewis."

Jewel felt tears bubbling in her eyes. Because she had wanted to be on Team Lewis with every bit of her being. Jackson had destroyed that for them with his professionally prepared prenup. What was professional about love? He didn't trust their love, and she didn't trust him. Not anymore. He would never get the chance to treat her like trash once he was through with her. She had been that kind of fool before. Never again.

She wanted to refuse to clink glasses with him. But that would create questions. She just had two weeks to go and the family would be in Antigua celebrating their parents. Once they arrived back home, Jewel would sit them down and tell them exactly why she was most definitely still on Team Dawson. But for now, she lifted her glass and toasted to Team Lewis.

5

Jackson hadn't prayed in a long time. He believed in God and all, he was just too busy for all the pomp and circumstance. But as he sat at the table with his dad, Jackson silently prayed that Jewel would keep her word and join them for dinner. In his mind, if Jewel showed up, then he still had a chance.

"Where is this soon-to-be daughter-in-law of mine?"

Jackson was a junior, although he hated admitting that to people. He was more like his mother than his cheating, irresponsible father. But his mother had died a few years back, and the old man was all he had left. If only they had thought to get him a sibling before the cheating started and Mom couldn't stand the sight of him anymore. Yeah, if he had a brother, he'd been hanging out with him, instead of Jackson senior and Vivian, his dad's fourth wife.

"She'll be here. I just need you on your best behavior. Jewel comes from a good family. I don't want her worrying about the family she is marrying into."

His father almost spit his water out of his mouth. He put down the glass. "Boy, please, Jewel don't care nothing 'bout your family just as long as you can pay them bills. I told you, money talks and all that other bull can go 'head on somewhere."

"That's a good one, baby." Vivian wrapped her arm around her husband. "You always coming up with witty sayings."

Jack smiled appreciatively at the compliment. "I got a million of 'em. You didn't think my son was the only smart Lewis man at this table, did you?"

"Baby, you're not only smart. You're also handsome." Vivian leaned forward and kissed Jack. "Your son looks a lot like you."

"I know all that. He got the money, but I gave him the looks." Jack sounded irritated. "I could have been rich too. Junior ain't the only one that's got a mind for business. Ain't that right, Junior?"

Here we go. It was about to go down. Jackson thought that his old man would at least wait until dinner was served before reminding them how having a son and getting divorced ruined his life. But evidently not.

"Hey, sorry, I'm late. There is too much traffic in this city." Jewel sat down next to Jackson. She said hello to Jack and Vivian.

"It wasn't always like this," Jack told Jewel."

Jackson had just planted a kiss on Jewel's cheek. She turned back to Jack. "Excuse me?"

"The traffic. When I was a boy growing up in this city. A lot of these streets weren't even here. This city used to be filled with trees. Then we got basketball and football, and suddenly, Charlotte was the place to be. Nobody likes trees anymore, they're bulldozing them all over the place."

Jewel smiled at Jack. "We're not going to complain about sports since that's how Jackson makes his living. And I guess I won't complain about all the trees that have been knocked down since I make my living selling the houses that are now being built as they clear away the trees."

"Girl, I didn't know you were a realtor." Vickie's voice was loud and shrill. "Jack's been promising to buy me a house for the last six months."

Jewel pulled her card out of her purse. "Let me know when you're ready to look. I can show you a few houses."

"Won't be no time soon if I don't get my hands on some cash. Like I was telling Vivian before you sat down, I had dreams of being a businessman just like Jackson. But I got stuck paying child support and alimony. So, I couldn't just go off and dream, I had to keep a job, so the gov'ment didn't lock my black behind up."

The waitress brought the menus. Jackson rubbed his hands together. "On that note, why don't we order our meals so I can make sure my wonderful father gets some of that child support back."

Jack laughed as he opened the menu. "If you think dinner is going to pay me back for how the system stripped me and gave your mama half my check, then I better get to ordering steak and lobster and a couple to-go meals."

Jackson snatched his menu off the table. Put it in front of him and let out a long suffering sigh.

"You okay?" Jewel put a hand on Jackson's arm.

"I'm good." He kept the menu up, not wanting to let her see his face. Because then she'd know just how ticked he was. But her hand on his arm was doing wonders for his mood. As long as Jewel was with him, he could get through this meal with his father. Jackson hadn't been on good terms with his dad since in a moment of weakness, he let his father work for him at the agency.

Jackson's mother had just died, and his father had acted like it mattered to him. Jackson thought that father and son could build something great together. His father knew this city like he knew his name. So, Jackson let him scout clients from the local high schools. The man over promised unsuspecting kids and had even charged a few of them for representation. When Jackson found out, he immediately fired his father. It took him an entire year to straighten out the mess his father created. Now they only saw each other two or three times a year, and even that was too much for Jackson.

They ordered their food, then Jewel stood. "I'll be right back."

Jackson took her hand in his before she walked away. "I like this dress. Is it new?"

"Matter of fact, it is. I ordered it a few weeks ago, but it just came in."

"Orange is your color bae. I think I'll buy you a few more outfits in this color."

She pulled her hand away from him. "I can buy my own clothes, Jackson."

As Jewel turned to go to the bathroom. Vivian got out of her seat. "That's a great idea. I need to go to the lady's room too."

Jackson's plastered smile dropped the moment Jewel rounded the corner toward the bathroom. He leveled cool, steely eyes on his father, the man who was supposed to watch out for him when he was young and help him grow into a man. But instead, Jackson Albert Lewis Senior had been too busy running after women and complaining about the evils of child support.

"I'm only going to say this once. I don't want to be here. I've tried to forget that you are my father because you've been lousy at your job. But my Mama made me promise to work on my relationship with you. She wanted me to have somebody in this world to call family, but I don't need you. And if you bring up that pitiful amount of child support one more time, I will give it all back to you and dismiss you from my life."

"Son, it's not like that. I don't want that child support back. I just don't think you understand how hard things were after your mama divorced me. Do you think I wanted to be married four times?"

"You could have avoided all of that if you had just not slept with your secretary. Mom said the woman left her a note, telling all your dirty secrets."

Jack's eyes filled with shame. "I never loved anyone like I loved your mother. She lit up every room that she entered." Jack jabbed a finger toward the bathroom. "Kind of like that soon-to-be daughter-in-law of mine."

Jackson smiled at the thought of Jewel. He wanted to tell his father that things weren't great between him and Jewel. But he didn't have that kind of bond with his father. The man was just a little more than a sperm donor who had once loved his mother, but certainly not a confidant.

"Don't lose her, Jackson. The best advice a man like me can give is to tell you not to let anything or anyone come between the love you have for that woman. Because you'll spend the rest of your life trying to replicate something that you already had. But trust me when I tell you, nothing will ever come close to your first love."

The sadness Jackson saw in his father's eyes caused him to feel more compassion for his old man than he had in a long time. It was all those basketball games that Jack didn't show up for when Jackson was a teen that caused Jackson to become skeptical of his father. Then all the marriages and the complaints about child support that showed Jackson that he'd never be able to count on his father. But they did share one thing— the love for a woman who had once been in their lives, and maybe that was enough for now.

~~~

While Jackson was finding something redeemable about his father, Jewel was having the opposite experience with Vivian. As she stood at the sink, washing her hands, the woman started in on her.

"I like the idea of you helping us find our house. Then you'll get the commission." Vivian winked at her as if they were conspirators on the same team. "Us girls gotta stick together."

"I appreciate the business. Hopefully, I can find a beautiful home for you."

Vivian dried her hands as she stared at Jewel through the mirror. "But you probably don't care about no commission since you don' hit the jackpot by marrying a man with so much money."

Jewel's mouth opened in pure shock. Had Jackson put this woman up to saying something so crass to her? Jewel's eye widened in disbelief as she snatched a paper towel from the dispenser and dried her hands.

"I didn't mean to offend you. I was just trying to compliment you on snagging such a catch."

"I didn't snag Jackson. We met. We fell in love." She shrugged. "That's it."

Vivian nudged Jewel's shoulder. "Yeah, yeah, just how Jack and I did it. We fell for each other quick. But I ended up with the short end because my Jack don't have any money. Now, I'm not complaining because he's got this rich son. And since me and Jack don't ask for much, I figured the least Jackson could do is buy us a nice home. I mean, how would it look if the tabloids found out that a big-time agent like Jackson Lewis bought his new bride a three million dollar home but let his dad's new bride live in a two-bedroom condo?"

"Are you threatening us?"

"No, of course not. But I certainly don't think you're the type of woman who only cares about her own happiness. We're going to be family. So, I hope you care about mine and Jack's happiness too."

Hands on hips. "And you think I should tell Jackson how to spend his money?"

"Technically, it will be your money, too, once you marry him. And you know, us girls have to get what we can while the getting's good."

Jewel could not believe this was happening. Was she being punked? Where were the cameras?

She couldn't imagine herself spending Thanksgiving or Christmas with this woman. Just because Vivian Lewis was Jack Senior's fourth wife, that didn't make her any less a part of Jackson's family. Jack and Vivian would be a package deal in the Lewis family. A deal Jewel wanted no parts of.

Pushing open the bathroom door, she rushed back to the table. Her plate was there, But Jewel wasn't hungry anymore. Instead of sitting down, she spotted the waitress and signaled her. "Can I get a to-go box?"

Jackson stood. "Wait? What?"

"I can't stay, Jackson. I've got to get out of here."

"But you agreed to have dinner. You agreed to talk to me."

The waitress came back with a to-go box and boxed Jewel's food.

"I can't right now, Jackson." How could she talk when all she wanted to do was cry? Jackson had a horrible family. None of them knew the first thing about love and marriage.

Jackson looked from Jewel to Vivian. "What happened?"

Jewel didn't respond. She headed for the door.

Jackson caught up with her and opened the front door of the restaurant. "At least let me walk you to your car."

"Just go back inside and be with your family, Jackson."

He kept following. They reached her car and he turned her around to face him. "You're crying." Jackson wiped the tears from her face. "What happened in that bathroom? Talk to me."

Jewel sat her to-go box on the hood of the car. She wiped at her face as more tears spilled. She clenched her fist and paced the length of the car. "Your stepmother wants me to get you to buy them a grand house, because after all." She did air quotes with her fingers "we girls have to stick together."

"Vivian is not my stepmother. The woman is only ten years older than I am. And she and dad just got married two months ago. I don't even know her like that. This is only my second time in her presence."

"Well, you enjoy Thanksgiving dinners with that. Because I want no parts of it."

"Babe." He put his hands in hers and moved closer to her. "What has you so upset about Vivian scheming for a house?"

Taking a deep breath, Jewel leaned her head back for a moment and then looked into Jackson's deep, dark, sexy eyes. Her first mistake had been letting him get close enough to take her hand. The second mistake occurred when she looked into those eyes. He loved her, and she knew it. But Jackson didn't have any foundation from which he could conceive of a till-death-do-us-part kind of love. She backed away.

"I never wanted some mansion, Jackson. Never asked you to buy me some big show home."

"What?" He looked confused. "I thought we were talking about Vivian wanting a house."

"Yes but, she thinks I'm the same type of schemer that she is. And that I got you to buy me some fabulous house so I can lounge in it and be fabulous with no job because, according to Vivian, I don't even need a job after snagging you."

"I know you're not that kind of person. Do you think I'd want to share my life with a woman who was only interested in what I could do for her? I like that you're independent. Heck, if this agent thing don't work out, we might have to live off your commission checks."

Jewel knew he was trying to inject humor, but she wasn't in the mood. She took her food off the hood of the car and got in. "That's exactly why I don't want the house you want to buy. I can't afford it."

"But bae, you don't have to pay for it. I got us."

Starting the car, Jewel shook her head in disbelief. He didn't have her back if he was protecting himself for an easy out if things got rocky. "So, what am I supposed to do if I'm stuck in a house you bought while you're somewhere filing divorce papers?"

"You're overthinking things, Jewel. Why would I want to divorce you?"

"Oh, but according to you, 50% of marriages end in divorce, right?"

"Yeah, but why we gotta be on the losing end of that fifty?"

"Exactly my point, Jackson. My parents and grandparents don't believe in those statistics because they believe in lasting love. Can you say you believe that love can last forever?"

He hesitated before responding, that was all Jewel needed.

"Exactly. Just leave me alone. I need time and space." She slammed her car door and drove off.

6

"It's a go. Mom finally confirmed that dad has taken the week off for their anniversary."

Jewel was glad she had been home when this call came in. "Kayla, thanks for bugging them about this. I will admit, with as close as we were cutting it, I was getting a little scared."

"We kind of got that when you basically threatened me and Serena."

"I'm sorry I got so angry about it. But that probably had more to do with breaking up with Jackson than how I was feeling about you and Serena."

"We know that. It just wasn't a good feeling."

Jewel understood what Kayla was saying. The three of them had always gotten along and never had reason to question one another. Jewel didn't mean to imply that she didn't trust her sisters, but admittedly she did struggle with trust issues.

"Jewel, can I tell you something?"

"Of course, you can."

Kayla cleared her throat, hesitating only a second. "I've only seen you cry over a man one other time. You were a junior in college, home for spring break, and I was a senior in high school. To be honest, that was the reason I didn't attend my prom that year. I thought if a man can hurt you that bad, I wasn't rushing into a relationship like that."

"That's when you broke up with Ron? You never talked about it, so I didn't ask you what happened. Now I feel awful knowing that I caused that. I always liked Ron."

"It's no biggie, Sis. I focused more once I broke up with Ron. I made it through college on the Dean's List, and now I'm working on my event planning business."

There was more Jewel wanted to say, but she hurried off the phone because her mind began traveling back to a time she'd tried to forget. But Kayla's words caused everything to come crashing back down on her again.

His name was Barrington Lloyd. His family had money, but she never thought he looked down on her because she was attending college on a partial scholarship. Then the truth came out, and she'd never been able to fully trust anyone again, not even God.

~~~

"Do you think we can cancel my meetings for next week and then book me on a flight to Antigua?" Jackson wasn't giving up. He wasn't going to lose Jewel's love without a fight. By the time he was finished showing Jewel how much he truly loved and wanted to be with her, she would have to report him as a stalker to get rid of him.

Reece reminded him, "You're supposed to meet with that kid who got passed over for the draft."

Jackson snapped his fingers. "Give me the kids number and I'll put in a call." He had to do this personally because this preview workout had been scheduled as a favor to one of his top clients. It just wouldn't do to flake out on them. "What else is on the agenda?"

Reece reviewed the calendar. "Let's see… you have a dinner meeting with Coach Williams. Oh, but wait a minute." She marked on the calendar. "He asked to reschedule. Something about a family obligation."

"Perfect. Let's move him back a bit."

Reece wrote on the calendar as she continued looking for other entries. "You have two phone conferences for next week. You can handle those while you're out of town, or I can reschedule. It's up to you."

"Sounds good. I can do that." He handed Reece a piece of paper. "Please take care of these other items for me today. I'm going home to pack."

~~~

The Dawson family gathered in Bradley and Vanetta's living room. The parents sat on the light grey sofa. The sisters stood in front of their parents, grinning like they held the world's secrets in the palm of their hands.

"What y'all got there?" Bradley asked his children.

"I'm the oldest, so I want to speak first."

Kayla rolled her eyes. "We know you're the oldest, Serena. You don't have to keep telling us."

"So, I guess I should go second since I'm the middle child. But then again, the middle child is always forgotten, so maybe I should just sit down and let the oldest and the baby take over."

Bradley put his hand over his face and leaned back against the sofa. "Don't start that stuff again, Jewel. You haven't said anything like that since middle school. And I spent too many nights praying to God that you would never feel left out or forgotten in this family."

Jewel went to her father and hugged him. "I was just joking, Daddy. With a father like you, I could never feel forgotten." She went back to her sisters and nudged Serena. "Go 'head big sis."

"Okay." Lifting on the balls of her feet, with excitement, Serena looked from Kayla to Jewel and then at their parents. "You both have been wonderful parents. You have sacrificed so much for us. Helped put us through college."

Bradley smiled at his girls. "Scholarships helped."

"Thank You, Jesus!" Vanetta lifted her hands in praise.

"Yes," Serena agreed. "You guys had smart children, so we were able to get scholarships. But they were only partial, so you had to foot the rest of the bill. And we know how much you gave up to do that. So now that we are finally out of your pockets, we wanted to do something that lets you both know how much we appreciate having you as parents."

Vanetta turned to Bradley. "Did you know about this?"

He shook his head. "Not only do I have no idea what these girls have cooked up… I had no idea that they even noticed the things we've done for them. So, I'm kinda stunned right now."

"Daddy, you know we love you. Stop it." Kayla shook a finger at her father.

Bradley pointed at Kayla. "Look at that one. Looking all innocent and sweet. But she's still in our pockets, ain't she Netta?"

"Leave her alone, Bradley. The girl just started her business. It takes time to grow."

"Yeah, Daddy, you've got to let my business grow, and then you'll see. I'll be out of your pockets too."

Jewel waved the tickets she was holding in the air. "Can we get back to business? My goodness, you may be the baby of this family, but everything is not about you, Kayla."

Serena ignored her sisters and refocused on their parents. "Your thirty-fifth anniversary is in four days, and we have something for you."

Jewel handed tickets to her mom and dad. "You won't be driving to Myrtle Beach this year for your anniversary. We are flying you to Antigua for five days of fun in the sun."

"Oh my God, are you girls serious?" Vanetta jumped out of her seat. "Can you believe this, Bradley?"

"No," was all he said as he stared at the airline ticket as if he thought it would disappear if he took his eyes off of it.

"That's not all." Serena looked from Jewel to Kayla. "Should we tell them the rest of the surprise or just let them learn as we go?"

Jewel shook her head. "We've held this in far too long already. I still can't believe Kayla didn't rat us out by now."

"Hey."

"Sorry, Kayla. Jewel didn't mean it the way it sounded." Frowning at Jewel, Serena turned back to their parents. "You will be renewing your vows at the resort as well."

"What!" Vanetta grabbed her husband's hands, pulled him off the sofa, and started jumping around the room with him. She let his hands go and started waving her hands in the air. "Thank You, Jesus! Thank You, Jesus!" You heard my cry. You've always granted, even the secret desires of my heart." Then Vanetta stood there, in awe of a great God, and cried.

Bradley lifted praying hands to his lips. Tears threatened to burst from his eyes as well. He turned to his children. "You just don't know." Then the tears did come. He was so overcome with emotion that he couldn't find more words.

Vanetta watched her husband walk out of the room, head bowed, mumbling words of gratitude to the Lord. She then gazed lovingly at her children. "Let me explain to you girls how God used you, grown women, to be a blessing in our lives."

Wow, Jewel thought her parents would love the gift. She had no idea that her mother was going to make it a gift from God. I mean, come on, does everything have to be about the Holy One?

"Sit down, girls. Let your mama thank you properly."

They sat down on the L-shaped sofa.

Vanetta propped herself on the arm of the sofa as she took a deep breath. "Your father and I never had a wedding. We got married at the courthouse because we didn't have two pennies to rub together, but your father promised to make it up to me."

Serena nodded. "You told us that."

Vanetta continued. "From the time your father and I got married, we made plans to renew our wedding vows on our twenty-fifth anniversary. To tell the honest to goodness truth, I was the one making all the plans. Your father just couldn't bring himself to stop me. So, about two years before our twenty-fifth anniversary, I came to him and asked about putting the deposit down on the banquet hall I wanted us to rent. He told me that we couldn't afford to spend the kind of money I wanted on a vow renewal when we had two daughters in college and a third on the way. It just wasn't practical."

"This makes me sad. We knew you and dad gave up a lot, but I never knew you gave up so much for us."

"There's nothing for you to be sad about, Kayla. Your father made the right decision. I was just being stubborn, and if I must admit it, my pride got in the way because most of my friends had beautiful weddings. I was jealous of them, so I kept bragging about my renewal ceremony." Vanetta shook her head. "I got so mad at your father that I went to stay with my mom for almost a week."

Jewel had never known her parents to spend one night away from each other until the week she came home from college during spring break. Her heart was broken, she needed her mommy. But her mom wasn't home.

Jewel had waited three days in her room, she just wanted to talk to her mother, but her mother and father were feuding. About what, she didn't know. She only knew that her mother wasn't coming home. She'd never known her parents to argue like that. It had scared Jewel. She hadn't wanted to put more on the situation, but when her mother finally did come back home, Jewel was silent.

From that day to this, Jewel hadn't wanted her mother in her business. She was a grown woman now and could handle things herself. If only she could get Vanetta to stay out of her business because she didn't want to talk like that anymore.

"I was foolish, girls." Vanetta looked at each of her girls. "I wanted more than what we could afford, and I made your dad out to be the bad guy. But the moment I walked back into the house, your father took my hand, we stood together right in this very room. He promised me that if I gave up my dream for my children, he would pray every day for God to do something for me that would blow my mind."

Serena said, "That's why daddy gets you flowers every month."

Kayla had a thought. "Is that why he takes you to the beach every year for your anniversary?"

Jewel added, "And why he wants to get that country club membership for you?"

Vanetta nodded. "Your dad has been blowing my mind ever since I let my pride go and admitted to my friends that the Dawson's couldn't afford a vow renewal. Now my friends envy our relationship. Because you see girls, I never got the fairytale wedding I wanted, but I got a marriage and a true prince."

7

"There's been some kind of mistake. I don't know what's happening here, but I can't afford to pay for this, so we need to get this straight before we go to our rooms." Jewel stood in front of the registration desk at the fabulous Sandals resort in Antigua. They were in the main lobby of the Caribbean section. The place was even more beautiful than the pictures she and her sisters had viewed online. The sand, the beach, the pops of color with flowers everywhere you looked.

"They have me and your dad in the Mediterranean one-bedroom villa. It comes with a butler and a private pool. We have to go over to the main lobby in the Mediterranean section to pick up our keys." Vanetta just about jumped out of her skin as she described where she would be staying for the next five days.

Jewel waved her hands in the air. "No butler. We couldn't afford the butler, so we didn't add it to the package." Jewel turned back to the clerk at the front desk. Before she could say anything, her grandmother exploded with joy as she walked away from the registration desk.

"We've got a butler too. I've never had a butler." Priscilla Dawson handed the resort map to her husband, Marcus Dawson. She pointed at the villa they would be staying in. "We're stepping in high cotton now."

Stress lines appeared on Jewel's face. "There must be some mistake. Can you please check your system? I sure hope you didn't charge my card for all these upgrades and butlers."

The clerk shook her head while reviewing her computer screen, "No, ma'am. Your card wasn't charged. Matter-of-fact, we sent your deposit back to you."

Jewel sighed with relief. This was just a clerical error. No harm, no foul. They could straighten this out now and get everybody into the rooms that were originally ordered. "So, we can pay for the rooms now? Good, because we need to make a few adjustments. My mom and my grandmother's rooms are all wrong."

"The rooms have already been paid for ma'am. There is nothing owed at all."

"Jewel, stop bothering this nice lady. She said the rooms have already been paid for and you haven't been charged for it. Don't you see God's hand in this?" Vanetta turned to her husband. "Come on, let's get that shuttle to the Mediterranean lobby so we can get the keys to our villa."

Grandma Priscilla grabbed Grandpa Marcus's hand. "Come on, we're in the Mediterranean too, let's catch this shuttle with Netta and Bradley." Priscilla burst out laughing as they headed out the door. "Wait 'til we get back home, and I tell that snooty Mable Jones what our grandchildren did for us. A butler… my Lord."

Serena and Kayla walked over to Jewel after receiving their card keys for their room. "Cheer up, Sis. I don't have a butler."

Kayla held up her key card as well. "No butler for me either, and we're in the Caribbean area just like we planned. It's a walkout, and I'm poolside, so I'm sure I will love it."

Jewel wasn't ready to smile about any of this. She had made the arrangements herself; that's why the deposit came off of her credit card. So, she knew the rooms that each of them was supposed to have. They were supposed to split the bills three ways, and since Kayla was just beginning her new business and money was scarce for her, Jewel didn't want to fight with her sister at the end of this trip. "But will you love paying for all of this once whatever glitch in their system gets fixed? I'm in the Caribbean area with you two, but these people gave me a room with a butler. This is crazy. I'm not about to let these people jack up my credit report, charging me for stuff I didn't order."

Trying to calm her sister, Kayla said, "Look, Jewel, I have all the paperwork you sent me, which shows which rooms we originally booked. So, if they try to charge us for all these upgrades, we have proof that this is their fault, not ours."

"And maybe it's like Mama said, this is a gift from God. She and dad deserve this after all they gave up for us, so let's just go unpack and enjoy ourselves."

"But… but."

Serena grabbed one of Jewel's arms and Kayla grabbed the other. "I mean it, Jewel. We are on vacation as of right now, and I said, let's go."

"Oh, and because you're the oldest. I should just listen to you."

"That's right."

"Fine, let's go. But you are going to be the one talking with management when they come talking about 'there's been a mistake and here's the real bill,' ain't that right big sis?"

Nobody was listening to her, so Jewel gave up. She let her butler take her bags to her room and then walked out of the lobby with her sisters. "Are we walking or taking the shuttle?"

Kayla's eyes filled with excitement. "I want to walk. Just want to take it all in."

Serena wrapped her hand around her youngest sister's shoulder. "I'm with you. This place is too beautiful to be taking a shuttle, we need to walk the land."

Jewel joined them, but she still wasn't feeling it like they were. Things might look wonderful now, but there was always another shoe to fall, and it usually fell on her head. But she wasn't going to rain on anyone's good time today. They arrived on the property on Thursday, but for some reason, the business office wasn't open. But first thing in the morning, no matter what any of them had to say, Jewel was going straight to the business office and make them straighten all of this out.

"Have you ever seen so many palm trees and flowers in your entire life." Kayla's mouth just about hung open as she took in the scenery.

Serena shoved Jewel. "Come on, don't be a spoilsport. You have to admit that this place is beautiful."

They were walking in the sand now, almost to the Paton building, where Serena and Kayla's rooms were. Jewel's sandals sunk into the sand. It got between her toes and felt so warm as the sun beat down on them. And for the first time since the whole fiasco at the registration desk, she smiled. "This truly is a beautiful place. Can you imagine how mom and dad are feeling right now?"

"Like a king and queen," Kayla said.

Serena shook her head. "If I know Grandma Priscilla, she has already told Mama that she and granddaddy are the king and queen of the Mediterranean villas, and mama and daddy are Prince Bradley and Princess Vanetta."

That sounded about right to Jewel. Her grandmother had been Vice President of Operations at a company she'd worked at for forty years before retiring. Grandpa used to say that Grandma Priscilla bossed everybody but him. He claimed he wore the pants at home. And from what Jewel observed as they grew up visiting their grandparents, that was mostly true. Grandma Priscilla never wanted grandpa to feel less than, just because she had rose through the ranks at her company while he was a city bus driver until he retired.

One weekend when they spent the night at their grandparent's home, Grandpa Marcus came into the house; his uniform was dirty. Kayla ran over to him when he hugged her, she said, "Grandpa, you stink."

"I had to work on the bus after it broke down."

"You're all dirty, ewww," Jewel had said, and scrunch her nose when he tried to hug her.

Grandma Priscilla shook a finger at her. "Never despise a man who's putting food on the table and bringing a check home every week."

Jewel never forgot that comment. Yes, her grandmother was a force to be reckoned with. But she loved her man and would do anything to ensure his happiness. After Jewel dropped her sisters off at their spot, she continued on to the Poinsettia building, which was only two buildings away from her sisters. It was far enough that she had time to think and wish she could find someone to love like her father or grandfather, a man who would stick and stay. But Jewel always found herself on the losing end when it came to love.

Here she was on a gorgeous island, at a romantic resort without her man. So instead of feeling hopeful, she wanted to cry. Jewel's room was on the bottom floor. She stood in front of the door, sighed, then put her card key in the door and let it swing open. Her eyes stretched the distance of the room. It was something out of a magazine. She had a huge four-poster king-size bed. There was a love seat at the foot of the bed. The room was so spacious that a sofa sat on the other side of the room.

Then she remembered the upgraded room fiasco. This place had a whole racket going on, they boost the price of your stay by giving you better rooms than you registered for, then smile and act like everything is all good. "Uh-uh, they not getting this off on me."

Closing the door behind her, she searched for the phone, so she could call Serena. She hadn't gone into her sister's rooms, so she needed to know what kind of upgrades they had. But as she picked up the phone, she peeked into the bathroom. "Dear Lord, is that a whirlpool?" It was a whirlpool. She called her sister's room. Serena answered. "Girl, do you have a whirlpool in your room?"

"What? Don't tell me they gave you a whirlpool. So, you've got a butler and a whirlpool? Something is up. I think you called and changed your room on purpose."

"I did not. Do you think I want to pay for all these upgrades? They have a love seat at the foot of my bed, another sofa over by the window. This room his huge."

"So, your room is bigger than mine too. Didn't those people at the registration desk know that I'm the oldest?"

"I wish you would have spoken up with me while they were throwing all these upgrades at us."

"You know what, I don't even care. I'm looking out my window right now, and I'm surrounded by flowers. I'm telling you, it's beautiful here!"

"Are you talking about the flowers that were in front of the building?"

"Yes, girl, I'm sitting on my patio and taking in the aroma of these colorful flowers."

Jewel walked over to her patio. She wasn't on the side of the island with green grass and flowers. Outside her patio was sand and clear blue beach water as far as the eyes could see. Beauty, pure beauty. "Oh, my Lord. I hate to tell you, Serena, but I have a beach view outside my patio." How in the world was she going to be able to leave this place in five days? It was everything… and much more.

"What! That's not right."

Jewel turned slightly and caught sight of the pink Amaryllis on the table. Amaryllis was her favorite flower. Only her daddy and Jackson had ever bought these flowers for her.

"Let me call you back." She picked up the vase to see if there was a card. No card. But everything was beginning to make sense now. The hotel hadn't upgraded them just so they could turn around and overcharge. What was happening to the Dawson family had been deliberate and planned out.

"It's beautiful, isn't it, bae." Jackson had quietly opened the door with his room key and was walking in, smiling at her like the good times were just getting started.

Jewel almost dropped the vase but regained her composure. She sat the vase down and stared him down like she was plotting where to hide his body. "What are you doing here? How'd you get a key to my room?"

"Our room," he corrected.

"She pointed toward the vase. "You sent these, didn't you?"

"Since you're still wearing that engagement ring, I think I'm the only man that should be sending you flowers, right?"

"Do you know what you put me through? I've been so worried that the people at this resort were plotting ways to take my life savings. Giving us villas and look at this room I'm in. My Lord, Jackson, why do you have to throw your money around like this?"

"I thought you'd be happy."

"You thought I'd be happy that you upgraded all these rooms. I can't afford stuff like that."

"I bet your mom and dad are loving their villa."

"Of course they love it. My mom thinks that God is showering down blessings on them. Now I have to tell them that Mr. Big Shot's just throwing his money around like he's at some strip club making it rain for the honeys."

"I'm not trying to be a big shot. And I have never made it rain for any 'honeys' at a strip club." He did air quotes when he said honeys. "I'm just trying to show you how much I love you."

She wanted to scream at him. The man had no clue. "Throwing money at a situation isn't how you show your love. You show it by being there every day. Even on the tough days. Even the I-don't-want-to-be-around-you days." She threw up her hands in aggravation. "What am I going to do with you?"

He stepped to her. Pulled her in his arms. "Love me, Jewel. Just love me."

He smelled so good. He was wearing Versace Eros. She bought him that fragrance for Christmas because of the blend of sweet and salty notes. "Don't you think I want to do that?"

That cologne was removing her resolve. The mix of mint, lemon, vanilla, and cedarwood that kept her inhaling his intense masculine, refreshing scent was assaulting and dismantling her senses.

She was born to love this man. There was no other way of explaining her existence on earth.

But he didn't want real lasting love.

He wouldn't be able to deal with problems that arise in a marriage. Would Jackson have prayed and waited for me to come to my senses and return home after leaving him because I got angry about canceling our twenty-fifth vow renewal like daddy did?

Would Jackson be the type of man to hold down whatever job he could, just so long as he brought home a check to support his family, not caring what the world thought? Or would he turn tail and run the moment things got tough and rough and hard. In Jackson's world, divorce comes easy. Divorce was simpler than sticking and staying.

But he felt so warm and comforting. His arms around her waist was giving her life. This man was everything and more. She could stay in his arms forever if only the rest of the world didn't exist. If only prenuptial agreements and men with four wives and husbands who gave up way too easy didn't exist. She could never trust that he would be there for her, not the way she needed him to.

As the saying goes, fool me once, shame on you, fool me twice, shame on me. But Jackson wasn't the one who fooled her the first time. Even so, she couldn't let him get this off on her.

Backing up, putting space between them. Space away from his smell, his touch, his here-today-gone-tomorrow kind of love. "Again, I ask, why do you have a key to my room?"

"We are engaged, Jewel. I thought you and I could share this room together. After all, it is the honeymoon suite."

Her eyes widened. "You did not put us in the honeymoon suite. Why would you do something like that? We are not married, and you are not sleeping with me while my parents and grandparents are at this resort with us. What were you thinking?"

"Look, babe, I messed up. I know I messed up. But I'm trying to fix it. Please let me fix this."

She waved an arm around the room. "How are you going to fix this? Do you really think putting me in the honeymoon suite and paying for my parents and grandparents to stay in a villa this week is just going to fix things between us?"

"I thought it was a start." He cracked a nervous smile.

But Jewel was not amused. "I sell houses, Jackson, but I have never been for sale."

Wiping the sweat from his top lip, Jackson stared at her like she was a puzzle, and he was trying to fit the pieces together. He took a step towards her but stopped. "I don't know what to say or do with you anymore. I thought you'd be happy with the upgrades, that's why I did it. I'm not trying to buy your love. I thought I already had that. Don't you still love me, Jewel? We couldn't have run out of love this soon."

She saw the look of pain that etched across his handsome face. A face she thought she'd be waking up to every morning. His mustache tickled her nose when they kissed. Jewel would remember that feeling for the rest of her life.

"Okay, wait a minute." He lifted a hand, trying to pause the situation. "You don't have to answer that yet. Hang out with me today. Let's just enjoy ourselves in paradise. How about it?"

She couldn't refuse him. "Lead the way, Jackson. After everything you've done, we might as well enjoy ourselves."

8

They headed out for a walk on the beach. Jewel was in a yellow, red, and orange striped sundress with tan sandals. Jackson wore a pair of shorts with a white t-shirt.

"It's beautiful out here, Jewel. This is the kind of place I'd like to take you on our honeymoon."

"Oh, I thought this was our honeymoon." Her eyebrow lifted.

"Okay, maybe I went a bit far in getting us the honeymoon suite. I can move us over to a villa if you'd like that better."

She shook her head. "I'm sure that's more expensive than the room I have now. So, no."

"Why do you worry about money so much? I have more than enough to take care of us."

Putting her hand to her chest, she stopped walking. "I'm not the one worrying about money. I didn't give you a prenuptial agreement, did I?"

Jackson took her hand and continued walking down the beach. "I like it here."

Jewel was trying to build a wall to insulate her from all that Jackson was to her. But when he put his hand in hers, she softened. They were, after all, in Antigua, at one of the most romantic resorts in the world. And they were on a beautiful beach walking hand in hand.

"Me too." And just like that, a silent truce was made between them.

"Hey, are you hungry?" Jackson pointed toward an eatery on the beach.

The restaurant was the Bayside. You could eat inside or on the terrace with a view of the sand and water. Jewel and Jackson chose a table on the terrace. They sat on white chairs under a red umbrella.

Jackson ordered the Mahi Mahi and Jewel ordered the shrimp and salmon. They laughed and joked as they enjoyed the ocean breeze. The food was delicious and filling. Jewel got so full that she needed a nap. But instead of going back to the hotel room, Jackson purchased a private cabana for them to lounge in.

It had a straw-roof and looked like a gazebo with two lounge chairs that were so comfortable they could have been beds. Curtains that blocked out the sun, which enabled Jewel to take a nap.

When she woke, Jackson was staring at her. "What?" She touched her mouth. "Was I drooling?"

"No."

"Then why you staring like that?"

"Don't blame me if I think you're something to look at, blame your parents. They created you."

The butler walked over to their cabana. He stopped in front of Jewel. "A Daquiri for the lovely lady."

Jackson laughed. "See, he thinks you're beautiful too."

"Shut up, Jackson." She turned to the butler. "I'm sorry, but I don't drink alcohol."

Jackson took the glass from the butler and sat it next to Jewel. "I know that. I ordered you a virgin daquiri."

"Ah, thank you." She sipped her refreshing drink.

The butler then handed Jackson and iced tea.

As he walked away. Jewel gigged. "I can't believe we have a butler."

"Hey, only the best for my woman. And don't you forget it."

A few more sips. "Was I snoring?"

"I'll never tell." Jackson had merriment in his eyes as he teased her.

She loved to see him happy. Loved just spending time with him. "So, what else you got for me. Are we going to lay around all day or what?"

Looking at his watch, he smiled up at her. "While you were sleeping, I ordered an excursion. I hope you don't mind."

"That depends on what it is. I certainly don't want to do any kind of swimming today. I just got this hair done; I'm not trying to deal with no snap back the first day at the resort."

"How about a horseback ride?"

"Horseback? We're on a beach."

"Where they do horseback rides. I've already booked it for us, so put your shoes back on and let's go."

"Why not? Let's do this. An hour into their horseback ride, Jewel was so glad that she and Jackson were on this excursion. They saddled up and then trotted along as their tour guide took them on a journey to some amazing places.

The horseback ride took them from the beach to the historic Fort James area. They dismounted from the horses and walked around the property. The tour guide let them see the eighteen-century cannons that could fire over one and half-mile distance. This area was fascinating to Jewel, who loved every minute of the history classes she took in college. She hadn't known anything about Antigua, though. She enjoyed discovering that Fort James had been built by the British in the eighteen century to protect the capital of St. John.

Construction on the fort began in 1706 and most of the buildings were completed by 1773. The fort had been named after King James II of England. However, the saddest part about viewing historical landmarks is when you see the disrepair of some of the places. And Fort James's fortified walls, although some still remained, a good portion of the wall had fallen down on different sides. The buildings that had once housed about seventy-five soldiers were now hollowed out and about to collapse.

"Thank you for bringing me here. I'm loving every minute of this adventure." Jewel's eyes were wide as she scanned from the green grass to the mountain side and then over to the sea.

Jackson helped her back on her horse. "You don't have to tell me you're enjoying this trip if you really don't like it. I'm a big boy, I can handle it."

"Jackson, this is me you're talking to. When have I ever held my tongue about any situation?"

He appeared to think for a second, then said, "You really like it here? I thought for sure you'd be upset that I picked a tour of a ruined old fort that its only claim to fame is its eighteen-century cannons."

"And weren't those some glorious cannons." She smiled at him, then leaned down from her position on her horse and kissed him.

Climbing onto his horse, Jackson had this goofy grin on his face. "Well, that settles it—no new house for you with an exercise room, theater room, and even a golf room. No, I'm going to buy you an eighteen-century house with only half a roof left and three good walls still standing. We'll rebuild it together."

"You know, that actually sounds like fun." She'd relish fixing up an old Victorian and truly making the house their own. But she didn't have long to romanticize living in an old drafty Victorian because they were now headed to Runaway Beach.

They actually got to ride the horse into the beach water. "Oh, my goodness, this is so fun!"

"It is, but your dress is getting wet." He reached out for Jewel's hand and once they connected, their eyes locked, just for a moment. But long enough for his heart to beat a new pattern. Then he had to concentrate so they could trot the horses out of the water without falling in... while holding hands.

Jewel was exhausted; they had been in the hot sun all day. And now she had to get dressed for dinner with the family, but all she wanted to do was take a nap.

"Go ahead and lay down. I'll wake you up in forty-five minutes. You'll have plenty of time to get dressed."

Jewel glanced at the clock on the end table. It was ten after five. Dinner was at seven. "Okay, but you can't fall asleep."

"I'm good. I have to get ready for a meeting."

She looked at him skeptically. "What meeting? I thought you were staying here for the week."

If he wasn't mistaken, it sounded like she wanted him here with her. Progress. "I've got a kid coming to Antigua to run some drills. I scheduled the gym at the school down the street. It shouldn't take long, but I promised Aubrey that I would give this kid a look. I hope you don't mind."

"Not at all, can I hang when you go?"

"If your family doesn't have anything planned for you, I'd love for you to go with me. Now lay down and get some sleep."

Jackson pulled his laptop out of his bag and sat down on the sofa, which would be his bed for the next few days. Before he opened his laptop, Jewel was curled up in bed, snoring. It was a light, girly kind of snore. He could live with it for, oh… maybe the rest of his life.

Jackson set the alarm on his phone before strolling through his email to find the stats on Brent Lloyd.

Brent's stats were pretty good, 19.8 points per game, 6.4 rebounds, 4 assists per game, and he had a 33% three-point field goal rate. Jackson had seen numbers like this from some coming out of college. If history was a predictor, Brent would go on to be an All-Star NBA player. He just wasn't getting noticed because everyone had Zion Williamson fever.

Stats were one thing. But Jackson needed to see this kid on the court. If he liked what he saw, he would begin working with coaches to get him a try-out. Brent should be thankful that his father had a timeshare in Antigua and that they were able to get out here this week; because things would start moving fast with the draft come next month.

His eyes drooped. He leaned his head against the sofa pillow, fell asleep, and didn't wake up until the alarm on his cell phone went off. Yawning, Jackson glanced at the time on his phone. He jumped up. "Jewel… Jewel. It's time to get up."

"No! I'm not ready to go. I'm not even hungry." She shewed him away.

Jackson pulled the covers off of her. "Oh no, you don't. You are not getting Vanetta ticked with me. Get out of this bed right now, Jewel."

Jewel laid there as her eyes came into focus. She rubbed her eyes. "Dang, you are really scared of my mother. She is not that bad."

"You never had to sit and explain yourself to her like I did. So, don't tell me she's not that scary."

"What did you have to explain to my mother?"

He'd said too much. "Jewel, just get out of that bed and get dressed."

"Oh, so now you're the boss of me." Jewel stretched, yawned, then climbed out of her king-sized bed. "This bed is too comfy. I could have slept through the night."

"I don't want to hear it." Jackson stood and rubbed his back. "I'm too tall for this sofa, and it's already started in on my back."

"Don't be a whiner. I'm sure we can get a bed rolled in here for you." Jewel went into the bathroom, jumped in the shower, and then put on another sundress.

Jackson took his time in the bathroom and came out refreshed and ready to go. Jewel was wearing a lime green sundress. He just so happened to have a pair of green shorts, with a matching button down shirt, so he put that on.

They had reservations at Kimonos Oriental Cuisine. All the Dawson's were seated around an eight-seater table when Jewel and Jackson arrived. Jackson held the seat out for Jewel.

"So, Jackson, you simply must come to our villa in the morning for breakfast. I'd love for you to see the place."

"I wish I could, Mama Dawson." Jackson sat down next to Jewel. "I have meetings tomorrow that begin first thing in the morning."

Bradley frowned. "You track my daughter down on this beautiful island, and you're not going to spend any time with her? Is that how it's going to be once you're married… traveling to exotic places that your money can pay for just so she can watch you work?"

"Daddy, that's not fair to Jackson." Jewel put a hand on Jackson's arm. "He rearranged his schedule so he could be here with us this week to celebrate your vow renewal. But he couldn't get out of this one appointment because the people followed *him* here."

"The meeting is on the other side of the island, sir. If I could have gotten out of it, I would have." Jackson turned loving eyes on Jewel as he finished, "And I can assure you, I have enjoyed every moment I've spent with your daughter since I arrived."

A hot plate was embedded at the head of the table. The chef arrived at their table and lit a fire. Then things got a little wild as the chef juggled the cooking utensils while taking their orders. The chef took out all the ingredients he needed to make their requests. He then flipped a shiitake mushroom into his hat. He even cooked some shrimp and flipped one in Jewel's mouth.

"Do me, do me," Kayla waved to the chef. He flipped a shrimp into her mouth as well.

Jackson leaned back in his chair and relaxed. He wouldn't be grilled any further tonight. Not with all this fun and the beautiful view of the sea that surrounded them.

"Let me introduce you to my grandparents."

"I'd love that." Jewel's grandparents lived in Florida, so he'd never had the pleasure of meeting them face to face. And had only spoken with the grandmother twice over the phone. They got out of their chairs and walked to the other side of the table.

"Grandma Priscilla and Pop-Pop, I wanted to introduce you to Jackson. He's—"

Jackson held out a hand to Pop-Pop. "I'm her fiancé. Nice to meet you, sir."

"Call me Marcus or Pop Marcus since you'll soon be part of the family." They shook hands.

Jackson nodded, then hugged Priscilla. "We've talked a couple of times on the phone, but I'm so glad to finally meet you."

"The same here, son. The way my granddaughter talks about you. I knew I'd see you in the flesh one day." Priscilla then got out of her chair and kissed Jackson on the cheek. "Welcome to the family." She said for everyone to hear, she then leaned close to his ear and whispered, "And thanks for my villa."

Jackson and Jewel sat back down as plates of teriyaki beef, ginger-infused chicken breast, and peppery shrimp were passed around the table. At the same time, fried rice and veggies were placed in the middle of the table for everyone to serve themselves.

Jackson couldn't help himself, he moaned like he'd found the greatest pleasure on earth. "This food is mmm-mmm. Get in there, girl." He nudged Jewel because she was staring at him, rather than eating her food.

"It is good, Jackson. But you don't have to act like it's your death row meal."

He cut a piece of his chicken and put it in her mouth.

"Oh, my God." Jewel savored the chicken and then chewed every morsel until it was gone. "You weren't lying." She took her knife and tried to cut another piece of his chicken. But Jackson moved his plate.

He pointed to the chicken on the table. "Get your own."

Jewel turned to her father. "Daddy, don't you share your food with Mama?"

"Don't start your mess, Jewel." Vanetta wasn't having it. "It's a whole plate of chicken right there in the middle of the table. I agree with Jackson. Get your own."

"I sure do." Bradley cut half of his chicken and put it on Vanetta's plate.

Vanetta rolled her eyes. "You're just encouraging her to be a brat."

Jewel turned back to Jackson and scrunched her nose. "See, you're just being selfish." She reached for the chicken plate.

Jackson grabbed it. "Oh, I'll show you selfish. He ran around the table with the plate.

"Bring it back, Jackson. I want some of that chicken." He kept going. "If you don't stop, I'm going to eat all of your shrimp. And we both know how much you love shrimp."

He stopped. Took his seat and handed her the chicken. "I lost my head for a moment. Where's the shrimp?"

Everybody at the table laughed as Jackson began shoveling shrimp onto his plate.

Grandma Priscilla smiled with great joy as she gave Jewel and approving look. "You're going to enjoy your life with that one."

As Jackson ate his shrimp and kidded around with Serena and Kayla, he hoped that Grandma Priscilla had called it right.

9

Early in the morning, Jewel and Jackson went to the exercise room to work off some of the delicious food they ate all day long and into the night the day before. They started with the treadmills.

Serena and Kayla walked in. Serena patted her stomach. "We can't eat another thing before working out in here for at least two hours."

Jewel laughed as her sister waddled over to the elliptical. "Why do you think Jackson and I are in here at seven in the morning." Jewel also patted her stomach. "Too much."

Jackson increased the speed on his machine, started jogging. "Stop all that talking and crank that machine up."

"Oh, you think you're doing something." Jewel increased her speed a notch above Jackson's and started running."

Not to be outdone, Jackson upped his speed three notches and gave up his jog for a run that would rival Usain Bolt.

"Stop showing off." Jewel reached across his treadmill and turned his speed down.

"You didn't know that I was All-Star in track. So, next time you try to outdo me, you might want to google me."

Jewel shook her head. "Whatever." She got off the treadmill and joined Serena on the elliptical. Hollering over at Jackson, "I doubt you were ever a mountain climber. So, come show me what you got over here."

Jackson waved her off as he made his way to the weights. Kayla joined him.

"I'll spot you," she told him.

"I'd love that little sis." Jackson laid down on the weight bench. "Put twenty-five on each side."

Kayla did as commanded. Jackson lifted the barbell about ten times.

"My turn." Kayla laid down on the bench when Jackson got up. She lifted the barbell once and then got up. "I can't."

Laughing, Jackson removed the weights and added ten pounds on both sides. "Your sister would not have admitted that the weight was too heavy."

"She's the competitor in this family. I'm the cheerleader."

"Jewel wasn't a cheerleader?" He'd never asked her but had assumed she had been. Jewel had the body of a cheerleader.

Kayla shook her head. "She wasn't interested in cheerleading. She played volleyball and was a praise dancer at church." Kayla did her reps then got up.

Jackson was about to sit back down when Kayla stopped him. "I wanted to thank you for what you did. I didn't want to upset Jewel or Serena, but the truth is, I didn't have my third of the money for this trip. You saved me from looking like a total flake to everyone."

He gave her a quick hug, muffed her head with his knuckles. "I'm glad I could help."

"And I'm glad that you're going to be my brother."

"What are you two talking about." Jewel wiped the sweat from her forehead as she waited for their answer.

Jackson laid down on the bench and waited for Kayla to hand him the barbell. "Kayla just told me she loves having me for a big bro."

"I sure do."

He stood, walked over to her. "And what's this about you being a praise dancer? You never told me about that."

Jewel looked away. The smile left her face. "Just something I used to do when I was a kid."

"Dance with me." Jackson grabbed Jewel's hands and tried to twirl her around.

She pushed him away. "I'm not in the mood for your games this morning, Jackson."

As he watched her walk away from him. Jackson found himself wishing that Jewel was as enthusiastic about having him for a husband as the other women in the Dawson family were about having him around. He wasn't giving up. Jewel was the one for him. If his mother was still alive, she probably would have pulled a switch out of the backyard and beat him with it for even thinking about a prenuptial agreement.

He still remembered her telling some friends about how his father had the nerve to complain about alimony and child support. She'd said, "If he had kept his behind at home where he was supposed to be, he wouldn't be sitting in that raggedy apartment with empty pockets."

With Jewel for a wife, Jackson fully intended to keep his behind at home, so did he even need a prenup?

~~~

After the workout, Jackson left for his meeting, and Jewel, Serena, and Kayla walked over to their parent's villa for breakfast and to meet with the wedding coordinator.

The butler brought them eggs, bacon, sausage, and pancakes. Jewel dug in. "There goes that workout."

"Tell me about it," Serena agreed. "I should have just slept in."

Bradley said grace over the food. "Dig in everybody. We've got a big day ahead."

Jewel didn't hesitate, she was starved after her workout. "Dad, did you and grandpa get a chance to pick the suites you'll be wearing to the wedding?"

"Not yet. Your mom has to pick the colors before we decide on a suit. Pops and I have a meeting this afternoon with the tailor."

Jewel was so excited for her parents. There had always been a bit of regret in her mother's eyes whenever she mentioned getting married at the courthouse. She had never told them about her disappointment in not being able to have a renewal ceremony for their twenty-fifth anniversary, but Jewel somehow knew that this vacation, coupled with the vow renewal, would bring joy to her parents' hearts. They hadn't stopped smiling since they arrived in Antigua.

Jewel admitted to herself that she was so thankful for having a man like Jackson. Someone who didn't mind sharing his wealth to make others happy. But that only made her question that whole prenup thing. Jackson was a generous man... sometimes too generous. So, why would he play her so cheap like that?

The doorbell rang. Vanetta jumped up. "They're here. Oh, my goodness, I can't believe this is happening." She opened the door and allowed the wedding coordinator access to the villa.

"Good morning Mrs. Dawson, I trust your morning is going well."

Practically giddy, Vanetta couldn't stop smiling. "Everything has been perfect. And your call last night was the icing on the cake. We are so ready to design my wedding, aren't we, Bradley?"

"Yes, ma'am. If you say we're ready. Then we are ready. I'm not about to get in your way."

By the look on her dad's face, Jewel could tell that he was truly happy that his wife was finally getting her wedding. He'd gotten in her way ten years ago, but there was no way he was going to interrupt one moment of her giddy, good-natured joy.

Looking over all the choices in patterns, linen, and colors, Vanetta turned to her husband. "I really like grey and peach together. I know it's not being done much anymore, but a girl wants what she wants."

Bradley squeezed Vanetta's arm as he leaned closer. "Then it is grey and peach. I'll call the tailor to see if he can fit Pop and I in something grey."

"Don't forget about Jackson, Dad. I think he'd love to hang out with you and Pop-Pop."

Bradley squared his chin as he glanced over his shoulder at Jewel. "Is he even going to show up, or am I just adding his name to our fitting list because he's a big spender?"

With a sharp intake of breath, Jewel's hand went to her neck like she was searching for some pearls to clutch. "Daddy, I've never known you to speak of anyone in such a manner. Jackson really wasn't trying to show off with his gesture to all of us. He just wanted to do something nice for us."

"I understand that. And I have no problem with thanking him for the gesture, but I'm not going to hold my tongue. I've got a problem with any man who gives a daughter of mine a prenuptial agreement to sign like she's just another business transaction to him." He shook his finger at Jewel. "He never told me nothing about a prenup when he took me out for that fancy lunch, or I would have told him to shove his proposal where the sun don't shine."

This time it was Vanetta with the intake of breath. "Bradley!"

"I mean it, Netta. All of y'all might be fawning over that boy, but I can't think of anything worse than a man giving the woman he loves a prenup."

Jewel could think of a few things that were worse. And if her daddy was this upset over a prenup, she would never tell him about her greatest nightmare. Just wouldn't do to see her daddy in jail.

"The boy don' went Hollywood," Grandpa Marcus said, adding fuel to the fire.

"Exactly!" Bradley turned to his wife. "That boy's got a lot to learn if he wants to marry my daughter."

"Then let him tag along with you for the fitting, it will be a good time to teach him, won't it?" Vanetta's arms folded across her chest as she waited on her husband's response. "You are not going to ruin this weekend for me, Bradley. I've waited too long—"

"Don't get on your soapbox, Netta. Fine, I'll take the boy with me." He left the room to call the tailor.

Jewel glared at her sisters. Keeping her voice low so her dad couldn't hear how furious she was. "Which one of you blabber mouths told daddy about the prenup?"

Kayla shook her head. "I didn't say anything to daddy. I promise."

Serena stood and did a cross of her heart, but Vanetta stopped her. "We don't swear to God about nothing in this house. Just let your yes, be yes, and your no be no like the Bible says."

"Okay, well, I didn't say nothing to nobody, and you can take that to the bank whether I swear to it or not."

Jewel believed Serena, her big sis had held onto other secrets, so there was no reason for her to start blabbing now. "Then how did he find out?"

"I told him. I just didn't think it was right the way that young man treated you. And I thought you broke up with him anyway?" Grandpa Marcus said.

"I did, Pop-Pop. But that's not what we're talking about right now. How on earth did you find out about the prenup?" Jewel was clueless until her grandmother confessed.

"I told him."

When Grandma Priscilla fessed up, Jewel knew exactly where the information had come from. "Why didn't you tell me that you knew, Mama?"

"I didn't want to get in your business. You're grown. I was sure you'd make the right decision."

"And what's the right decision. If someone could please tell me because I just don't know."

Kayla spoke up. "Jewel, it's obvious to all of us that Jackson loves you. He made a mistake, just forgive and go on and marry that man."

"I don't even want to hear from you, my little snitch of a sister. Because I know you're the one who told Mama. You're always running everybody's business to Mama. That's why I don't tell you nothing."

"Okay, girls, don't start none, won't be none," Vanetta told them in the same manner she used to bust up disagreements when they were kids.

"But Mama, you know that ain't right. Kayla always telling everything she knows." Jewel rolled her eyes, so fed up with her sister right now.

"I do not. I didn't tell Mama that you and Jackson are shacking up together this week." Kayla's hand immediately went to her mouth.

Jewel shot daggers at her sister, then turned to her mother. "He's sleeping on the sofa, Mama. After he spent all this money on ALL OF OUR hotel rooms." Jewel exaggerated the words as she glared at Kayla. "I didn't want to make him spend even more money."

"Good girl." Grandma Priscilla nodded her approval. "Like my Mama used to tell me, they rarely buy the cow when they're getting the milk for free."

Jewel had great respect for her mother's and her grandmother's stance on morality. It was outdated, but she'd never disrespect them by shacking up, but the milk had been spilled a long time ago, she just didn't know how to tell them her truth.

"I think I've picked all the items needed for the vow renewal," Vanetta told them. "Let's grab that pitcher of lemonade and sit around the pool. You all have got to check out this plunge pool that's right out back."

10

The ladies made their way to the plunge pool while the men sat in front of the television.

"This is really nice, Mom," Jewel said as they sat down around the pool.

"Me and your daddy came out here and swam last night. Might get another swim in tonight." The smile on Vanetta's face said it all.

Serena lowered her head. "Mom, could you not. We really don't want to even know about you and daddy like that."

Grandma Priscilla laughed. "How do you think you got here?"

"That's what I tell that girl. And does she think I'm not going to know what she and her husband do in the midnight hour?"

"I don't think we have to concern ourselves with that for a while because I have no prospect insight. Let's all just get in Jewel's business and leave me and my non-existent sex life alone." Serena pointed at Jewel.

"What? I don't have anything to tell either. Heck, I don't know if Jackson and I are even getting married."

"Don't be no fool," her grandmother said. "You better marry that man and go on and live your best life."

"But granny, he wants me to sign a prenup. I can't agree to that." Jewel took a sip of her lemonade as she tried to figure out how she'd gotten into this conversation in the first place.

Vanetta waved her hand as if spatting a pesky fly. "That boy loves you. He'll change his mind about that prenup, mark my words. But that's not what you need to worry about."

Should she bite... don't bite. But as usual, Kayla kept the conversation going.

"Don't just tell Jewel what she needs to know about marriage. Tell us all, Mama."

Vanetta smiled; that was all the encouragement she needed. "You girls know that I never had a wedding, but I had a marriage and a good one. Your father and I both gave our lives to our wonderful Lord and Savior six months after we got married because we basically wanted to kill each other. But Jesus made all the difference.

"So, if I could give one piece of advice to each of you. It would be to make sure that you keep God in your marriage."

What kind of advice was that? How does one keep God in their marriage?

Kayla refreshed her glass with lemonade and then sat down at the feet of her mother. "You've said that to us before, but what does that mean? How do you and dad keep God in your marriage."

Exactly, Jewel wanted to scream. But since she was the only one of the Dawson clan who wasn't a regular attendee at the Glory of God Ministry, she decided it would be best to keep her thoughts on the low-low.

Leaning back in her seat like she was a woman with the patience of Job, Vanetta lifted her head toward heaven, then she turned back to her daughter. "I know that you girls have been well educated. Got your college degrees and have forgotten some of the things your father and I tried to instill in you." She glanced toward Jewel. Jewel turned away.

"But just know that marriage is not like lavish vacations and sweet nothings all the time. Trouble comes to every marriage. Some even get to the breaking point."

"You ain't lying," Grandma Priscilla chimed in. "When I went back to work once my boys were in high school, everyone thought it was because I couldn't wait to run something, tell somebody what to do. But the truth was, we were broke.

"My Marcus felt terrible that he couldn't keep up with the needs of the house and the needs of the kids. And as I started climbing the latter on the job, I know it did something to him, tore him down a little. But I never cared about how much money he made. Marcus has treated me like a queen every day of our marriage.

"So, I prayed and asked the good Lord to show me how to mend my husband's pride. How to make him feel like the man I knew him to be."

Jewel's eyes widened. She put a hand on her grandmother's arm. "That's why you stopped me from telling Pop-Pop he stunk that day he came home from work all dirty from working on that bus?"

Priscilla nodded. "Marcus had taken on some extra shifts because he knew I was planning to retire. We were paying off the house that year, so I wasn't going to let some snot-nose little girl," she lovingly touched Jewel's nose and then squeezed her cheek. "Come into my house and make my man feel less than the man God created him to be, just because there was a little dirt on his uniform."

"Wow." Serena looked impressed. "And prayer guided you to do that for Pop-Pop?"

"Yes, ma'am. The Lord showed me what Marcus needed. I didn't always rise to the occasion, but I think I got it right more than I messed it all up."

"Having Priscilla as a mother-in-love was a big help to me. Because I learned about praying for my husband and even for myself when I didn't feel like being the wife my husband needed. Believe it or not, my beautiful daughters, you will not wake up every morning happy and joyful that you are married. Some days you'll just feel stuck and out of luck. That's when you have to remind yourself that God doesn't deal in luck. He deals in blessings.

"He can bless your marriage if you let Him. Years ago, I turned my closet into my prayer room. I go in there when your father has made me so mad that I want to walk out and never come back… but when I begin to pray, God always shows me myself. He is so merciful that He never allows me to stay mad for long. And I thank the Lord for giving me a husband who is able to deal with the wife God gave Him. And I'm sure he does a lot of praying himself."

Kayla nudged Jewel. "See, it was good that I told mom what happened with you and Jackson. If I hadn't, Jackson wouldn't have come to dinner last week, and we wouldn't be enjoying an even better time at this resort."

Jewel turned toward her mother. "You called him? Did you grill him about the prenup?"

Vanetta shook her head as she told Kayla, "Your sisters are right, you can't hold water." Vanetta then answered Jewel. "No, I didn't mention that silly little document. I only invited him to dinner because Kayla told me how hurt you were about ending your engagement. So, I knew you didn't want things to end with you and Jackson like that."

"But I also didn't want my family butting into my business. Y'all are so embarrassing."

"We don't want to embarrass you, so let's stop talking about that. I have something else to ask you."

Something in her mother's eyes told her she wasn't going to like what was coming next. "What can I do for you, Mama?"

Vanetta seemed to hesitate. She steepled her hands. "I've been praying about this, and I hope this is the right time to ask you. But really I don't have much time left because the wedding is in two days."

Jewel's head leaned to the left as she waited for her mother to get to the point.

"I was hoping you would dance for us during the reception."

"What?" Jewel frowned. "I haven't danced in years, Mama. Why would you even want me to do that and ruin your reception?"

Vanetta walked over to her daughter. She put both hands on Jewel's arms and looked deeply into her eyes like she was trying to discover some secret. "God gave you a gift. You are a praise dancer. The most anointed dancer I've ever seen. God's glory is revealed through you when you dance, and your father and I would be honored to see a little bit of that glory at our reception."

Maybe that's why she hated dancing. The glory was gone. Shaking her head, Jewel got up and headed for the door. "I can't with y'all right now. I've got to go."

"Wait, don't leave." Serena caught up with her.

"What now?"

"Dang sis, stop trippin'. We have to get fitted for the dresses mom is about to pick for us."

"Just tell me where to go to be fitted, and I'll take care of it later." Jewel left, even though she had every intention of spending the day with her family picking out wedding stuff. But in truth, watching her mother pick out china, linen, colors, and flowers was making Jewel feel some kind of way about the whole thing. And why was everyone suddenly reminding her about praise dancing?

She tried to shake it off. Her parents didn't need her in a bad mood while they were experiencing so much joy, but then her father's voice invaded her thoughts as she made her way to the lobby so she could get a cab. Bradley Dawson rarely raised his voice at his children. So, she knew he was heated. Which made Jewel wonder what kind of fool would defend a man who'd treated her like a business transaction?

~~~

Brent Lloyd was nice on the court. Jackson couldn't believe his good fortune. If it hadn't been for the injuries Brent suffered two years in a row, he would have already been a sure bet for the draft.

Aubrey Watson was some kind of angel or something. Because he was making big things happen in Jackson's life. First off, Aubrey was going high in the draft. Teams that don't select this kid from one to three will live to regret it. But those spots were pretty much locked in. But Jackson was a good judge of potential.

If he had never seen Aubrey hooping it up at the YMCA with some of his high school buddies, Jackson would have missed his chance to get to know this kid. He would have missed out on meeting Jewel because he never would have been at Aubrey's father's church on mother's day if he hadn't been trying to get Aubrey's parents to let him represent Aubrey when it was time for the draft.

And now Aubrey introduced him to Brent, a kid who was as nice as D-Wade in his prime. Teams were sleeping on Brent. But Jackson was about to wake them up. He read the boy's profile and knew that Brent had one big problem that teams didn't want to deal with. But the problem had nothing to do with his injuries. Jackson was about to see how bad this family wanted Brent to go to the NBA. "Okay, Brent, that's enough."

Brent took the ball to the hoop. Dunk. When his feet touched back down on the court, he shimmied. "Did you see that? That boy is the coldest! That boy is a superstar!" Brent kept bragging on himself as he dribbled the ball over to the bleacher where Jackson sat with Brent's family.

"You got this, Brent. Didn't I tell you that you were the next MJ? You got this." Barrington Lloyd the third, put his hands on his son's shoulders like he was giving a quick massage.

Mary, Brent's mother, turned to Jackson. "What do you think? Can he make it in the NBA?"

Dismissing his mother and becoming his own hype man as he bounced around in front of them. "Oh, I'm going to the NBA. Them fools don't know what's coming at them."

Barrington the fourth, Brent's older brother got hyped to. "My kid brother got hops."

Jackson stood, he turned to the mother. "Since you asked. Brent has skills. He's better than tons of guys already in the league. But his stature is lean, and he breaks easily."

Forehead frowns appeared on the faces of all three Lloyd men.

"My son will change the game when he gets to the NBA. Look at Steph Curry."

The big problem stood in front of him, claiming his son was as good as Steph Curry. But Jackson thought this could be a teaching moment. "That's exactly who I want you to look at." Jackson walked around Brent, pointing out the leanness of his body. "Steph had been thin like Brent, and he got hurt a lot, but he has continued to work on strength training. I'm sure someone has advised your son to do that."

"Yeah, but adding muscle weight is just going to slow me down."

"If your son won't listen. If he just wants to brag about how great he is on a court with amateur players, then I can't help him. Because, he'll get to the league, no doubt. But will his career be over before it gets started?"

Barrington Senior looked like a man who hadn't taken no for an answer in a very long time. He was a show-runner, a shot caller, the HNIC. "You agents all seem to think you have Brent figured out. I'm working on a shoe deal for him right now. Yeah, didn't know that did you? This boy is special and trust and believe you'll soon be clambering for your cut."

Jackson was getting a headache. The daddy was running the show and would soon mess Brent's career up, if he hadn't already. "I don't advise you to do that just yet. Brent will not go high in the draft. Those shoes won't be worth much. But if he becomes something special in the league, that's when the shoe companies are going to take notice and shell out multi-millions for him."

Brent slammed the ball down, frustration etched across his face. "Everybody thinks I'm hard-headed and not listening to nothing. But I tried to bulk up. Drank that muscle milk, ate twice the amount I normally eat... nothing. I'm just a skinny kid who's going to get knocked around in the NBA, and there's nothing I can do about. Okay." With that, Brent stormed out of the gym.

For the first time since Brent came off the court, Jackson smiled. He told Brent's father, "If you stay out of it, I think I can work with your son."

"What do you mean, stay out of it?"

Mary came to stand next to her husband. "He wants you to let him do his job, Barry. And if you really want what's best for Brent. You'll listen this time."

That's right, you tell him. Jackson wanted to punch the air, he was so excited that he had somebody in this family on his side. Brent had too much ego. But he got it from his daddy. The kid's one show of doubt came when he slammed that basketball down like it had broken his heart and stormed out. He could work with Brent because, for all his bluster, the kid knew his limitations. The question was, could he work with the daddy?

11

Jewel kept herself busy until Jackson finished his meeting by checking out a few of the shops along the street where she and Jackson were going to have lunch. This had been a terrible day for her, snapping and yapping at everybody. The morning had started off good, getting in a little exercise. Then boom, she became like the devil. But that might be unfair, her mother never liked when they referred to themselves like that, said the devil was a whole other beast. He was cunning, conniving, and pure evil — nothing like her children.

Retail therapy was what she needed. And this multi-colored jumpsuit was giving her new life. She pulled it off the rack and tried it on. "Oh yeah, I can rock this." Jewel paid for the jumpsuit and headed to the next shop.

Her phone beeped. It was Jackson telling her that he was on his way to the restaurant. She put her phone back in her purse and continued to the dress shop just to look around. She doubted she'd have time to try on anything she might see, but if she liked the place, she and Jackson could come back before they headed back to the resort.

This dress shop had wall to wall sundresses and hats, they had short dresses, some long, and some off the shoulder. Oh yeah, she was coming right back to this shop. And she would make sure

Jackson kept his wallet in his pants pocket where it belonged. He might be rich, but Jewel knew for a fact that he couldn't have more than a few million to his name, based on the clients he had.

A few million was certainly more than she had, but it still wasn't enough to be splurging on three million-dollar homes and extravagant vacations like it's nothing. If, and that was still a big if, she was going to marry him, she was going to teach him how to hold onto some of his money.

And once again, Jewel found herself being disgusted by the very idea of a prenup. Instead of trying to guard his money against a wife who might wants to leave, he needed to be making smart decisions with his money in the here and now, so he could have some serious bank.

She was so busy thinking about how she was going to fuss Jackson's trifflin self out for getting her daddy all riled up that she wasn't paying attention when she stepped into the restaurant. She tripped over the step and went headfirst into the back of the man who had been standing just inside the restaurant.

Jewel was thankful she didn't fall but felt bad for the man she ran into. She was about to apologize, but as she straightened, she found herself looking into the eyes of the devil. And Jewel felt certain that her mother would agree that Barrington Lloyd Junior was the straight-up antichrist.

"Oh, my God." She needed some holy water. She would splash it on him to see if he might just dissolve before her very eyes.

"Jewel. What are you doing here? I mean, how are you? How've you been?"

"Those are a lot of questions, which do you want me to answer first?" Jewel's lip curled as she stared at the man who had broken her heart, crushed her dreams, and even stolen two very precious things from her.

A woman walked up to Barrington. A very pregnant woman. She put her hands in his. "Our table is ready, babe."

Jewel noticed the ring on Barrington's finger. "You're married?"

"Yes," the woman answered joyfully for her husband, who hadn't been able to form the words.

"Expecting. I. See." The words were like a jab as Jewel floating them out into the atmosphere. She wasn't really talking to either one of them. Didn't expect an answer. Just had to say what was painfully obvious.

Jackson came to her, then put his arm around her. How she needed that strong, loving, always there for her arm.

"You made it." He kissed her on the cheek. "I hope you don't mind, but we're having lunch with the Lloyd family."

What did Jackson say? Did he just invite her to eat with the devil?

"Jewel." Jackson took hold of her arm. "Come on, hon, our table is ready."

She pried his fingers off her arm as she backed away from him. A text popped in from Serena. She glanced at it. "I forgot, I have to get back to the resort for our fitting. And daddy needs you for a fitting this evening, so please call him to get the time."

"Are you serious, Jewel? You came all the way over here just to turn around and leave like this?"

She couldn't breathe — honestly couldn't breathe. If she didn't get out of this restaurant, she was going to pass out. She hated the look on Jackson's face. He thought she was trying to hurt him. But the truth was, she was hurting so bad the roof could fall down on her head, and it wouldn't feel any worse than how she was feeling this very minute… she's pregnant, and they were holding hands. Happy.

Her voice caught — sound was having trouble squeezing through the lump in her throat. "I've got to go."

Spinning around, Jewel pushed through the door and got out of the restaurant as fast as her legs could take her — wishing she was a bird. If she was a bird, she would fly away. Fly away and hurt no more. Tears sprang to her eyes as she got in the cab. She didn't want the cabbie to think he'd picked up a lunatic. Stop. Stop. Stop, she commanded her tears, but they weren't listening.

"You okay, ma'am? Did someone bother you while you were shopping today?"

She shook her head. She wished her problem was that a local had tried to snatch her purse or something. She could have fought back, call the cops. But how did she fight against self-loathing and shame?

When she was younger, Jewel read in the Bible about Jacob wrestling with an angel and declaring that he wouldn't let the angel go until he blessed him. The angel had told Jacob that he would be blessed because that night, he had wrestled with God and won.

She wished she could wrestle with God and get Him to take the stain of shame away. Maybe she'd dance again, even lift her hands and praise the Lord like her sisters and her mother did every Sunday.

But what was the use, there was no forgiveness for people like her. Life would never go right for Jewel, not ever again.

~~~

Jackson was befuddled, confused, perplexed. Jewel was the best thing that had happened to him. He was like Percy Sledge singing When a Man Loves a Woman, out here willing to spend his last dime just to hold on to her love. But Jewel needed to show him something.

What she pulled at lunch today wasn't cool at all. How could she make him look so foolish like that?

Jewel had texted him with the time and place to meet up with her dad for the fitting, but she wasn't answering her phone and hadn't bothered to explain why she played him like a stocker she couldn't wait to get away from this afternoon. Did he need to take a hint and leave her alone? How many times would she have to give back his engagement ring before he realized that Jewel just wasn't into him like he was into her?

Frustrated as he was, Jackson didn't want to mess up the planning for the vow renewal. So, he made his way to the tailor shop, hoping that Jewel's dad would cut him some slack since he was trying to be apart of the festivities and not spend the entire week working.

But the moment Bradley saw him, he basically smirked as he said, "Oh, so you were able to pull yourself away from your important business?"

"Yes, sir. I handled everything, and I won't be bothered with any business for the rest of the week." Jackson made circles of his thumb and index finger and raised them to his eyes. "I'm focused."

Marcus clamped a hand on Jackson's back. "Good. Good. Just remember, son, family is more important than anything else this world can offer us."

"I'm trying to keep that in mind. I really am, but this is all new to me."

The tailor started taking measurements. As Bradley stretched out his arms and let the tailor work, he turned to Jackson. "Let me ask you something. Do you know what it means for a husband to love his wife like Christ loved the church?"

What the what? Jackson didn't know anything about Christ or His church for that matter. His mother didn't find Jesus until he was grown about two years before her death. So, how did Christ help her?

This was not the time to air his grievances about this so-called high and mighty God. So, he simply told him, "I didn't grow up in church like Jewel did, sir. I don't know much about Christ's love."

"Well, son, that's where you need to start," Marcus told him. "You see, the Bible tells us that a house divided against itself cannot and will not stand."

Jackson shrugged. "We're not divided. Jewel doesn't go to church either."

The tailor finished with Bradley and started taking Marcus' measurements.

"If you bothered to read the Bible, you'd know that what you said, don't make sense." Bradley shook his head as he tried to explain the reality of the situation to Jackson. "See, the Bible says that if you raise your kids up in the Lord when they are old, they won't depart. Which means Jewel is coming back. You ready for that?"

What was he supposed to be ready for? He didn't understand the big deal.

Marcus chimed in. "My wife is my rock. That woman showed me the benefits of having a praying wife. And then I got the hang of it and started praying for her as well. I knew she thought I resented her high falutin career, but I prayed for her each time she was up for a promotion. Wanted my baby to shine, whether she was cooking me a good home cooked meal, or taking charge at that job of hers."

Jewel had told him about her grandmother working her way up the corporate latter to VP before retiring. She'd also told him that her grandfather was a bus driver. Jackson just wasn't sure if he'd be okay with Jewel making more coins than him. "You didn't have a problem with her making more money than you?"

Marcus gave an honest answer. "I did at first. My pride got in the way. I'd been taking care of the family for so long, but suddenly my money wasn't long enough. I don't even know what changed or why it became okay with me. Just one day, I was no longer bothered by it." Marcus shrugged. "God has a way of fixing things if we let him."

"What you gon' do when y'all get ticked off with each other?" Bradley asked like he was quizzing him.

Jackson and Jewel were going through something now. He was trying to keep the peace so... "I don't know, maybe go sleep on the couch until things cool off."

Bradley and Marcus gave each other a look and then rolled their eyes.

Jackson pointed at them. "What was that look for? What did I say that was so wrong?"

Bradley gave him an I-pity-you-look. "When does a king come off his throne to sleep on the couch?"

Defensive because he was sleeping on the couch now, Jackson challenged, "What's so wrong with sleeping on the couch? My father does it all the time if he and one of his ladies are arguing. He says the time apart helps the situation cool down."

Bradley shook his head. Them Dawson men had that I-pity-you look down pat. "Moving a man away from his own bed is like moving a man's heart away from his home and his obligations."

"Yeah, but won't that just make her even angrier? How are you supposed to work things out if you don't let stuff cool down first?"

"That's where prayer comes in. How long you think your wife is going to stay angry when she sees you praying about the situation? Bradley asked.

Marcus added, "And it doesn't hurt to start acting right. Maybe come home with some flowers."

"Say them I'm-sorry words," Bradley added.

"What about her? What if she's the one wrong?"

"Not your job to worry about her. Give your wife to the Lord and let Him convict her. Your job is to keep peace in your home. You got that?"

Jackson heard Bradley, but this stuff sounded foreign because his father never said anything like this to him. It was just, 'sleep on the couch and wait 'til things cool off.' Maybe that's why he was on his fourth wife. Because things didn't always cool off like that. Jackson was pondering that as they left the tailor shop and ran into the Dawson women.

Vanetta put her arms around her husband. "We just finished our fitting, and I'm starving. You ready for dinner?"

"We just finished our fitting, and I'm starving too." Bradley turned to the group. "Y'all want to walk the beach and find a restaurant to eat at tonight?"

The group nodded. "Sounds like a plan.

"Where's Jewel?" Jackson asked the women.

Serena shrugged. "She bailed on us. We thought she was still with you."

Jewel had told him that she had to leave their lunch because she had to get to the fitting. Now he discovers that she didn't even get fitted with her sisters. What was really going on? Was he supposed to say, 'I'm-sorry' to a woman who had lied to him?

12

Jewel was in the fetal position with her face turned to the window staring out at the sea wondering what it was like to just float away and take her problems with her. She wasn't one of those people who thought that no one would miss her or care that she was no longer around. But she did wonder if they would continue to want her around once they knew her truth.

So caught up in self-pity, Jewel didn't hear the door open. But she did hear the contempt in Jackson's voice when he said, "I don't believe you, all snuggled up in this bed enjoying a nap after how you lied to me."

His voice dripped with venom. Maybe Jackson had already discovered her secret and hated her for it.

"Don't ignore me, Jewel. You owe me an apology. I'm not letting you get away with what you did."

All those years ago, she'd thought she'd gotten away with it. Thought no one knew or suspected anything different…

"Turn around and face me!"

Jewel didn't have the energy for this fight. She pulled the covers over her head, hoping that he would just go away. Their love was doomed anyway. Everything and anything she touched was doomed forevermore.

Jackson turned on the light and snatched the cover from the bed. He stood in the way of Jewel's ocean view. "You are going to talk to me. I deserve an answer, I don't know what's going on with you, and I'm beginning to wonder…" His eyes bore into her, and he got a glimpse of her curled up in that fetal position, looking frightened like a ghost was chasing her. "Have you been crying?"

She put the pillow over her head. "Leave me alone."

Jackson climbed onto the bed and pulled her into his arms. "I'm not leaving you like this. You looked terrified. Tell me what's going on. What's got you like this?"

"You said you knew about my lies. Why are you here? Why are you acting like you care about me when Barrington told you what I did?"

"Barrington didn't tell me anything. What does he have to do with the fact that you told me you were going to the fitting with your sisters, but never showed up? Then I find you here looking like the world is closing in on you." His eyes widened. He got off the bed, sucked in his breath like he was preparing for a blow. "What's going on with you and Barrington?"

Oh God no, she could tell Jackson was thinking that she'd cheated on him with that devil. No, she couldn't leave him to think something like that. She took the pillow from her head and sat up. "Nothing is going on with me and Barrington. Not anymore, anyways."

"Are you lying again?" Jackson sat down on the ottoman at the foot of the bed. His shoulders slumped as his hands lifted to his face. "Never thought I'd be catching you in a bunch of lies so soon."

She heard his words and understood that in Jackson's world, the shoe eventually dropped, he just didn't think things would fall apart for them so soon. She had disappointed him. But he didn't know the truth.

Jewel sat down next to Jackson on the ottoman. "I dated Barrington when I was in college."

"So what are you telling me? Seeing him today was too much for you because you're still in love with him?"

If she had eaten lunch today, she probably would have vomited it up at the suggestion that she could still be in love with a devil-like Barrington Lloyd the fourth. "Not at all. Truth be told, I despise him. I never wanted to be on the same side of the earth with him ever again in my life, and then he was suddenly standing there with his wife, and she was…"

"Say it, Jewel. What are you trying to tell me?"

But she just couldn't form the words.

Looking into her eyes, Jackson tried to figure her out. "Were you jealous because his wife is pregnant?"

Jewel stood. She walked over to the patio doors, looking out at the water she thought about floating away again. Take the pain away. Take the shame away.

"Talk to me, Jewel. You owe me an explanation."

Pulling at her hair, she turned to face him. To face the truth, her truth, that she'd been running from. What she'd done. "They were happy about it. It made me sick to my stomach that he had the audacity to be happy about a woman carrying a baby for him."

She couldn't breathe. Heaving. But not breathing.

Jackson grabbed her and shook her shoulders. "Stop acting like this. You don't have to be jealous of their baby. You weren't meant to have a baby with him. We'll have kids. As many as you want."

Shaking her head and putting her hands over her ears, she screamed at him. "I don't deserve another baby. I want the baby that

I killed. Can you bring that baby back? The one I destroyed all because the father didn't want me or it."

There, she had finally said it out loud. She was a murderer.

She was also drained and out of breath again. She needed to lay down and sleep. She needed to sleep the sorrow and shame away.

~~~

Jackson didn't know what to do. She'd called herself a murderer. Did that mean he was a murderer as well because he'd paid for an abortion a few years back himself? He and the girl had met up at a party and hooked up for one night. When she came to him three weeks later claiming she was pregnant, Jackson had serious doubts that the baby was his. But he'd given her the money she requested for an abortion without a second thought.

Now he wondered if that woman had expected more of him. Had she wanted him to want her and the baby as Jewel had hoped Barrington would have done? Had he left some woman to suffer over her decision like Jewel was doing?

He let Jewel lay down while he sat at the computer desk to check emails. He had to do something to take his mind off of the ugliness Jewel had just revealed to him. He didn't think less of her, but Jewel was harboring ill thoughts of herself for something that happened ten years ago. He would give her a little time to process everything, but they needed to talk this out.

Before dealing with work emails, he texted Vanetta and told her that Jewel wasn't feeling too well. They were going to eat in and call it a night. Then he sent out one more text before getting down to business.

After answering his emails, Jackson ordered room service for them. Added hot tea to the dinner request because Jewel loved green tea with lemon. She said it soothed her. When the food arrived, he woke her up. "Come on, hon, you need to eat."

Jewel stretched, yawned, rubbed her eyes. "How long have I been sleep?"

"Only about two hours."

Glancing at the clock. "It's almost nine o'clock. My family is probably worried sick about me. I haven't seen them since breakfast."

"I text your mom. Told her you weren't feeling well and that we'd stay in tonight."

"Okay, but let me text her myself, or she'll be coming over here bringing me some soup or something."

"Your mother is a trip," Jackson said, trying to lighten the mood.

"Don't I know it. But I love me some Vanetta Dawson and hate disappointing her."

"Yeah, I get it." He gave her some privacy so she could send her text while he took the lid off their plates and made sure she had just the right amount of lemon in her tea.

"Thanks for ordering something to eat." Jewel sat down at the table with him. "I really am hungry but didn't have the energy to even think about going anywhere."

"I got you, girl. You don't have to worry about anything when you're with me."

She tried to smile, but the light didn't quite meet her eyes. Jackson tried again. "Look, I know this has been an emotional day for you. Just eat and then we can take the tea out on the patio, watch the waves, and if you want to talk. That's what we'll do."

Jewel reached across the table and put a hand over his. "Thank you, Jackson."

Steak, potatoes, and asparagus were on the menu tonight. Desert was a New York style cheesecake. The meal was mm-mm delicious. When they finished, they took the cake and tea out to the patio.

Jewel stared out at the water and seemed to exhale.

Jackson told her, "While you were sleep, I texted Barrington Jr. and told him to blame himself for the reason I am about to decline taking his brother on as a client."

She gasped. "You didn't?"

"I did. But being for real, I don't like the daddy either. So, I've got two reasons to suggest they find Brent another agent."

"Brent?" She said it like a question like she was trying to remember something. "Barrington did have a younger brother named Brent. I think they have always been very close, even with the age difference."

"The kid is nice on the court too."

Jewel sighed as she took Jackson's hand in hers. "Let me ask you something? If there was no Barrington Jr. or senior, would you take Brent on as a client?"

He nodded truthfully. "In a heartbeat. With the right guidance, Brent can be something special. He'll never rival MJ like the father seemed to think, but he could be a hall of famer no doubt."

Then forget about me and both Barrington's and just think about Brent and what he could possibly be. You're a good agent, Jackson. Not because of the deals you close, but because you really care about those kids. Maybe Brent needs an agent like you."

"The only thing I care about right now is you. I need to know that you're going to be okay. The way you responded today after seeing the man's wife." Jackson shook his head. "I can't see putting you through that again."

She sipped her tea and kept looking at the sea. "It caught me off guard. It did. But only because back when we were in college, Barrington acted like my pregnancy was going to ruin his life. Like his father would disown him or something."

"I met the man. He probably would have."

"I was treated like the life growing inside me was nothing. Even though I knew better, I allowed him to convince me that abortion was our only option. And as soon as I did what he wanted, he cut off all communication with me. First, the baby was nothing, then I was nothing."

Jewel turned to Jackson and put the teacup down. "That's how I felt when you sent me that prenuptial agreement, like you were saying that I would once again be nothing the moment you were through with me. All you'd want was to dismiss me with as little fanfare as possible. Just sign here and go on about your business."

Jackson was stung by her words. Never in life had he ever wanted to make her feel like she was nothing. Not Jewel. Not the woman who was everything and then some to him. "I never meant to hurt you like that Jewel. That was not my intent. You've got to believe me when I say you could never be nothing to me. Even if we should part, I'd spend a lifetime regretting the loss of you."

Tears filled Jewel's eyes. "I don't deserve a man like you. I don't." She got up, took her plate, and teacup to the kitchen, then pretty much ignored him for the rest of the night.

Jackson was confused by her behavior. What more did she want from him? He'd just basically told her that she was everything to him. When Jewel went back to sleep, he was tempted to leave their room and go hang out at one of the night spots on the island. Maybe he could have a little fun with people who didn't mind having him around.

But then he remembered something Jewel's dad said to him. Something about a man loving his wife like Christ loves the church. What did that mean?

He couldn't call Mr. Dawson, the man could barely stand having him around as it is. So, he wasn't going to press his luck. Jackson sat down on the sofa and pulled out his smartphone. He googled 'loving a woman like Christ loved the church'.

The Gateway online Bible came up, and he clicked on it. It brought up Ephesians 5:25-33.

Husbands, love your wives, even as Christ also loved the church, and gave Himself for it;

That He might sanctify and cleanse it with the washing of water by the word. That He might present it to Himself a glorious church, not having spot, or wrinkle, or any such thing; but that it should be holy and without blemish.

So ought men to love their wives as their own bodies. He that loves his wife loves himself. For no man ever yet hated his own flesh; but nourished and cherished it, even as the Lord the church: For we are members of His body, of His flesh, and of His bones.

For this cause shall a man leave his father and mother, and shall be joined unto his wife, and they two shall be one flesh. This is a great mystery: but I speak concerning Christ and the church.

Nevertheless let every one of you in particular so love his wife even as himself; and the wife see that she reverence her husband.

When Jackson finished reading the scriptures, his head hurt. He was confused. How did Christ give Himself for the church? What did that mean?

He didn't know and had no one to ask, so he Googled it. That's when he discovered that the way Christ gave Himself for the church was by dying on the cross. Jackson wasn't that uneducated about church matters. He knew that Jesus died on the cross. He just didn't know that a husband should also be willing to die for his wife.

He'd just said that Jewel was everything to him. But was she give-your-life everything? And if a wife was supposed to be that tight with her husband, how come there were so many divorces?

What if there were more secrets to uncover? Would he still be able to love her and be willing to give himself for her?

13

Jewel was greeted by the devil even as she slept. He had black wavy hair, deep chocolate skin, and black unfeeling and uncaring eyes.

She stood in front of this huge house, nervous, excited, anxious. Today she would meet Barrington's family, and they would tell them about the baby. Before she could knock on the mahogany double doors, Barrington opened it looking just as nervous as she was. "That was fast," Jewel joked and smiled at him.

But Barrington wasn't smiling.

He grabbed her arm and pulled her off the porch toward the end of the circular drive way. "What's going on, are we leaving? Are your parents home?"

"I'm not leaving, but you are."

"What? But you told me to come and meet your parents."

"They don't want to see you. They don't want to know anything about you."

Jewel felt ill. She was going to throw up, she'd been throwing up a lot lately. She touched her stomach. "But… baby."

"Don't try that with me. How do I know that baby is mine? You're just trying to get your hooks in me because my family has money."

Her hand went to her chest, shoulders slumped as she inwardly shrunk. "It's me, Barrington. I don't understand why you're being this way." She had known Barrington since her freshman year in college. Dated him since her sophomore year and waited a whole year before giving him her most precious gift… her virginity.

His face softened but only for a minute. He reached in his pocket and took out a wad of money. He put it in her hand. "Take it. You shouldn't have to take care of some baby on your own, get an abortion, Jewel."

Some baby — their baby. He wanted her to kill their baby. He'd never said anything like that before. "Why did you tell me to come here if you were going to be like this?"

He didn't answer, just started walking away.

"Barrington! Barrington! Don't do this. You said we were going to be together."

"Don't call me. Don't bother me anymore," he threw the words over his shoulder as he walked in the house and shut the door.

She was left to stare at this humongous house with tan siding and rock overlay. The stonework was laid from the midpoint of the house all the way to the bottom, it went from the front of the house to the sides like a fort built to keep people like her out.

With a jolt, Jewel sat up in bed. That house. It was like the house Jackson wanted to buy. She had put Barrington's family home out of her mind because she'd never been inside, only stood on the outside like an interloper.

Looking around the room, she saw Jackson sound asleep on the sofa. She almost woke him to apologize to him for having such a visceral reaction to that house. There wasn't anything wrong with the house. It was the Barrington's. They were the kind of people who would treat you like your nothing. Throw money at you and tell you to go away. But not Jackson. Jackson would never treat anyone like that. But she didn't want to wake him because things were complicated with them right now.

As she laid in the bed trying to get back to sleep, she kept thinking about the unthinkable. The thing that she'd tried to block from her memory, but it still guided most of her decisions. It was the reason she and her mother's relationship had become distant. And why she and her sister's had problems at times.

If she was ever going to have any peace in her life, Jewel knew that she needed to get right with her family. So, when they got up that morning, she and Jackson got dressed and went to her parent's for breakfast.

Butterflies danced in her stomach as they walked in the villa. Her sisters were already there, fixing their plate. Jewel asked her mother, "Where's Pop-Pop and Grandma Priscilla?"

"All tuckered out. They are sleeping in this morning."

Jewel almost sighed with relief. She didn't want her grandmother hearing what she had to say. So, she was so glad that they would not be over for breakfast. Now she needed to figure a way to get her father out of the house.

She had been a little standoffish to Jackson since last night, but now she needed him. "Do you think you can arrange a golf game for you and my dad this morning?"

"I'll see what I can do." He pulled out his cell phone and stepped outside.

Serena rushed over to Jewel. Pressed the back of her hand to Jewel's forehead. "You don't have a fever, but you look like you fought your worst enemy and lost."

"You might be right," Jewel admitted, but then walked away from her sister. She went to the buffet table and started filling her plate.

Jackson came back into the house. Grabbed a plate at the buffet table. Bacon. Sausage. Eggs. "It's a go. I'll ask your father if he wants to join me in a minute."

"Thanks, Jackson. I appreciate that." As much as she wanted to smile at him, her lips wouldn't curl upward, only down.

Jackson moved close up on Jewel and whispered in her ear. "You don't have to do this. Most people never tell anyone after doing something like that."

She was whispering too. "You can't even say the word, Jackson. That lets me know that you're ashamed of me too."

"Then I must be ashamed of myself too. Because I paid for one."

Her eyes bucked like she couldn't believe that he had basically done the same thing she'd done. "Why didn't you tell me this last night?"

"You stopped talking to me, remember?" He threw it back at her.

"What's all the whispering about over there." Vanetta waved them over to the breakfast table. "Get on over here so we can eat."

Jackson turned from Jewel and headed over to the table. "I was just telling Jewel that I have reservations for golf this morning, and I was hoping that Mr. Dawson would join me."

"Golf!" Bradley's head swiveled in Jackson's direction. "How'd you get in? I called, but they told me the course was all booked up."

Jackson shrugged. "Someone must have cancelled."

Vanetta rolled her eyes heavenward. "Golf is Bradley's first love."

"Hush that fuss, woman. A man has to relax somehow. And besides, you and the girls still have a few things to iron out for the vow renewal service, right? You won't miss me around here."

Jewel sat down next to her mother, silently praying that she wouldn't make a big fuss about daddy leaving. Let him go, Mama… let him go.

"I don't care about your old golf game, Bradley. If you want to get in a round or two, that's perfectly fine with me. Just, please don't stay all day. We're getting married tomorrow, and I'd like a proper rehearsal and you know we're having our reception dinner tonight instead of after the wedding."

"We've been married for thirty-five years, Netta. And nothing on this earth would cause me to mess up this vow renewal ceremony for you."

Vanetta smiled at him. "Thank you, husband, then I'll see you at five for the rehearsal."

"I'll be back before then. Now everybody, bow your head so I can pray over this wonderful breakfast our butler brought to us this morning." He shook his head in wonderment. "Never thought I'd ever say butler in association with anything I was doing. This is just too much."

After breakfast Jackson and Bradley left for their golf game. The women changed into their swimsuits and lounged around the plunge pool in the back.

Vanetta turned to Jewel. "Jackson told me you weren't feeling well last night, but you don't look like you're doing much better this morning. I didn't want to say anything while your dad was here because I didn't want him worried about you. But do we need to take you to a doctor? Do you think you might have gotten food poisoning or something?"

Jewel sunk into her lounge chair, wanting to just disappear. But she knew she couldn't do that. Not anymore, not if she ever wanted to be free of this load she'd carried for so many years. She just didn't know where or how to begin.

"Jewel, I know you think I butt into your business too much. But that's only because you won't tell me anything. I can tell you're hurting. I just want to help. Please let me help you."

"I want to talk to you, Mama. This is just hard for me." The very woman that she hadn't wanted in her business since the day she made the worst decision in her life — was the one she turned to now so she could figure her way forward.

Kayla stood. "Do you want me and Serena to leave so you can talk in private?"

Jewel shook her head. "This involves you too, Kayla." A tear rolled down Jewel's cheek. "And I'm so sorry for what my actions cost you."

Confusion set on Kayla's face, "Cost me? You haven't done anything to me, except call me a blabbermouth. And I admit that I do tell Mama stuff from time to time, but that's only because you won't tell her anything."

Kayla sat back down. Vanetta turned to her middle child and put a hand on her arm. "You and I used to be so close. I don't know what happened, one day you just shut me out. But I'm still here for you. Do you hear me? Your mother will always be here for you, no matter what."

She had to face this. Had to get rid of this load of guilt and shame. It was too much to carry. Too hard to move forward. With a deep sigh, she began. "Last week, you mentioned the time you left dad because he'd told you that there wasn't enough money for our college educations and your vow renewal."

Vanetta nodded. "Not proud of how I reacted, especially seeing how God has truly blessed us for doing the right thing with what money we had."

"You thought that none of us girls noticed your absence that week and that it was no big deal because you and daddy worked everything out, and all of us girls finished college. But that was the week I came home pregnant, rejected, and scared."

"What?" Vanetta's head snapped back like a mighty wind rolled in and almost knocked her over.

"Barrington had promised to tell his parents about the baby, but instead, he hands me money for an abortion and tells me not to call him anymore. I came home because I didn't know what to do. Growing up in church, I knew that, first of all, sex before marriage was wrong. And that abortion was wrong because it is murder — unjustified murder."

Jewel put her head down. She was so ashamed of the choices she'd made. Choices that hadn't included God. Choices that she'd hid from the very people who love her unconditionally. "I was just twenty years old. And you and Dad were fighting. About what I didn't know, but I didn't want to cause any more problems." She glanced up at the faces of her sisters and her mother before putting her head back down and crying. "I was just so miserable."

"Oh, baby." Vanetta sat next to Jewel and pulled her into an embrace. "I'm so sorry I wasn't there for you. This is why the word of God admonishes against selfishness. We never know when someone else might need us while we're off doing our own thing."

"It's not your fault that I had the abortion, Mom. But I do wish you had been home that week so we could have talked about it. I was so miserable thinking about how I had let God down and let you and Dad down that I let myself believe that if I did what Barrington wanted, then that would solve the problem all the way around."

Serena took the seat her mother abandoned so she could be closer to her sister. "It didn't solve the problem, did it, Sis?"

Through the tears, Jewel shook her head. "As much as I tried, I never forgot what I did."

"I felt the same way for a long time, too," Serena admitted. "I wasn't home with you all during that spring break because I was with Carl making plans for us to move in together right after graduation. It was the biggest mistake of my life, and I never talked to anyone or asked for advice before rushing into something that doomed any chance he and I had at marriage."

Vanetta looked over at Serena. "I will admit, your father and I were livid once we discovered what you had done. But we knew you'd come to your senses. We just put you in God's hands."

Serena leaned forward, took her mother's hand, squeezed it. "Thanks for that, Mama."

Jewel had also thought that Serena's choice to move in with her then boyfriend had been a mistake, but Serena's mistake only hurt her, Jewel had also hurt Kayla, and she needed to make that right.

Setting her eyes on her baby sister, Jewel expressed her anguish. "When you told me that you broke up with Ron after seeing how miserable I was that week, I felt even worse. Because the way I was feeling that week had little to do with Barrington."

Kayla still didn't understand her sister. "What do you mean? You just told us how Barrington dismissed you and the baby. Surely you were distraught because of his actions."

"I was disappointed in him. Because I really did think he loved me. But I was distraught because I knew that what I had done would forever separate me from God. So, I'm sorry, Sis. Ron may have been the man for you, and to know that I ruined that for you just tears me up inside."

The four of them were all crying now, for what was once, and what was no more, and for what Jewel lost in the midst of it all.

As Vanetta wiped the tears from her face. She lifted Jewel's chin so that her head would no longer hang low. "I am so, so sorry that I wasn't there for you. I will never forget what my selfishness cost you." Vanetta was crying too.

"No, Mama, don't cry. I can't blame you for what I did. And I don't want you to blame yourself.

The four of them were crying and holding onto each other. Then Vanetta opened her arms wide, and each of them came to her for the hugs that only Mama could give. Vanetta wiped each face, just as she had done when they were little and came to her crying.

Jewel kissed her mother on the cheek. "Thank you for being here when I was ready to talk. And I'm sorry I did this here, right before we celebrate your anniversary."

Vanetta shushed her. "Okay, we all messed up. In life, we are going to get it wrong sometimes. But if I've taught you girls nothing during the years I had y'all at home, I tried to teach you about a God who loves, heals and forgives."

The girls nodded. But Vanetta was aiming at Jewel as she said, "Don't you know that God wants to remove the stain of sin and shame as far as the east is from the west for you?"

As a teenager, she had been in the dance ministry at church. Jewel had the love of God in her heart to the point where she'd do anything, go anywhere, and tell anyone about a God who wanted to forgive and save them from their sins. Because she believed that God could do anything. But that was before she, herself, had sinned and needed the forgiveness of a loving God.

"This is why you've stopped coming to church and stopped dancing, isn't it?" Serena shook her head. "I'd always thought that you believed the misinformation those college professors fed us, and that's why you only showed up at church every so often. But it was much deeper for you, huh Sis?"

"I just didn't think I belonged there anymore. God hadn't forgiven me, so why bother."

"But Jewel, have you ever asked God to forgive you?"

"Over and over, Kayla. But I had yet to feel God's forgiveness. I knew better, and I still sinned anyway. Maybe God doesn't have forgiveness for people like me."

"Uh-uh, baby." Vanetta placed her hands on both sides of Jewel's cheeks as she declared, My Bible says that God does not retain his anger forever because He delights in steadfast love. He has compassion for us, so He will tread our iniquities under His foot. He casts our sins into the depths of the sea. So, let me ask you something. If God can forget and forgive your sins, why can't you? Who made you better than the Almighty?"

14

While Jewel was trying to believe that a forgiving God could also forgive her, Jackson and Bradley were enjoying their time on the golf course. Jackson even confided in Bradley. "I read the scriptures you told me about… you know, about a man loving his wife like Christ loved the church and all."

Bradley was about to swing. He adjusted his body. Turn to Jackson. "What'd you get out of it?" Then swung.

Jackson put his ball on the tee. "It was heavy. I mean, I get the part about a man caring for his wife like he would care for his own body. But this thing about Christ giving himself for the church. Well, to me, the way Christ gave Himself for the church was that He died — was crucified even."

Bradley's eyes brightened as he looked at the young man. "You're beginning to see that being married is not this cakewalk, romantic scene twenty-four-seven that movies and commercials try to sell us on." Jackson swung, as Bradley added. "That's a good thing."

"How is that a good thing?"

"Because you'll go into marriage with your eyes open. You'll know that every day won't be sweet for you and Jewel. But you'll also learn how to die to yourself — die to that desire to walk out and call the whole marriage off."

"That's deep, Mr. Dawson."

Bradley put a hand on Jackson's shoulder as they headed back to the golf cart. "I like you, Jackson, you're a good man. But can I be honest with you?"

"I'd like that, sir."

"Until you learn how to walk with God and know how to pray my daughter through the situations and trials of life," Bradley shook his head. "I don't see y'all surviving marriage."

That stung, Jackson was just about to protest and assure Bradley that he was exactly the man that Jewel needed. He could provide for her, he loved her. He still wanted to be with her even though she'd been giving him the cold shoulder. What more did they need? But before he could open his mouth, the Lloyd family descended on them. And they looked like they were coming to split a golf club over his head.

"Jackson, you owe us an explanation," Barrington Senior declared.

"We're trying to enjoy our golf game right now. So, I'll get with you later." Jackson tried to rush Bradley to the golf cart. They were putting their clubs in the bag as Barrington Junior approached.

"Let me at least explain myself before you take your anger out on my baby bro. He's got nothing to do with what happened between me and Jewel."

Bradley swung around. "You know my daughter? What's going on here?"

"You're Jewel's father?" Barrington Junior stretched out a hand as if he was happy to meet Jewel's father. "I owe your daughter an apology for the way I acted when we were in college. If she would have stayed at lunch yesterday, I would have given it to her then."

Bradley hadn't taken the hand that had been offered to him. "What did you do to my Jewel?"

Jackson tried once again to usher Bradley away from the Lloyd men. "We don't have much time left, you know that Mama Dawson is expecting you back soon."

But Bradley brushed the arm Jackson put on his shoulder off. "I want to hear this guy out, Jackson."

"No you don't, Sir."

"This has something to do with my daughter. Then I want to hear it."

"My problem is my son." Barrington Senior jabbed a finger in Jackson's direction. "And this idiot is refusing to represent Brent all because your daughter got herself knocked up."

Bradley almost tripped and fell as he stumbled backward. "What!" He looked from Barrington Junior to Jackson. "My daughter is pregnant? Who's the daddy?"

~~~

Jewel wasn't a hundred percent yet, but she did feel as if some of the weight had been lifted. Her sister forgave her for ruining the budding relationship she'd had with Ron Goodman. Jewel finally, truly, all the way in forgave her mother for not being there for her during her time of crisis.

The girls were now taking a swim in the pool while Vanetta ordered lunch. Then all of a sudden, the front door swung open, and Jewel heard her father's booming voice as the door slammed behind him. She'd never heard his voice sound so angry, so hurt.

"Jewel, where are you? Come here this instant."

The voice she heard ricochet off the walls reminded her of the time she was in high school and had wrecked her mother's car.

"How are we going to pay for this?" He had demanded an answer from Jewel.

"Car insurance, duh," she'd answered flippantly.

"There's a five hundred dollar deductible on our car insurance, and now our rates are going up because you took the car out with only a permit. You should have waited for your mother like she told you."

She'd learned a hard lesson in finances that year. Her father made her get a summer job and pay back every cent of the five hundred dollar deductible. She hadn't crashed another car since. So, what had caused her normally mild-mannered father to be in such an uproar now.

Jewel and her sisters climbed out of the pool and went back into the villa. To Jewel's shock and horror, Barrington was standing in the living room. No. No. This isn't happening.

She turned to Jackson, who was looking just as miserable as she felt. "What's going on?" Actually, she had a feeling of what was going on, but she really wanted to know why this thing that she never wanted to happen at all was now going down in front of her parents.

"I tried to stop them, but your dad wouldn't listen to me." Jackson sat down and looked away like he wanted no parts of whatever this was.

"Dad," Jewel said slowly. "Why did you bring Barrington here?"

Bradley's nostrils flared as he looked back at Barrington. "He's got something to say to you. And I think it's high time he got to it."

Vanetta stepped into the six-foot space of distance between Jewel and Barrington. She held up her hands. "I don't think this conversation needs to be done in front of all of us. I'm going to cancel our lunch order."

Vanetta turned to her husband. "Let's all go out for lunch, so Jewel and this gentleman," she pointed toward Barrington, "can talk."

"I want to hear what this man has to say to our daughter. After what he told me, ruining my golf game like that. He better have a good apology."

"Daddy, please let me speak with Barrington. I'll catch up with you all later, okay." Jewel found herself praying that her father would back down. What girl wanted her father listening in while a man described why she hadn't been good enough for him.

Bradley sighed. He seemed to loosen up a bit. "If you're sure?"

Nodding. "I am Daddy."

As her family filed out of the villa, Jewel sat down next to Jackson. She invited the devil to have a seat across from them. Many nights, this man had tormented her dreams, but not once had she ever dreamed that he would come find her with hat in hand.

Barrington sat down. "Before I get started, I just want to make sure that you know I'm not here in order to get my brother the agent of his choice. I wanted to apologize to you for years, but never had the guts to do it."

Jewel wasn't in a charitable mood. She wanted him to eat every horrible word he'd said to her. "Oh, so all these years later, you realize that telling me you didn't want me or the baby and that your parents wanted nothing to do with me wasn't the right thing to do? Is that it?"

"I get that you're angry. I even understand why your father is so upset. Because if my little girl dealt with a knucklehead like me, I'd probably try to kill him."

So they were having a girl. Well, good for them. Maybe she should throw the wife a baby shower with the exact amount of money he'd given her to rid them of their child. "Okay, you're sorry. You've apologized, now you can go on with your life."

But Barrington shook his head. "That's just it. I hadn't been able to go on with my life since the day I let you walk away with abortion money in your hands. And whether you believe me or not, I did want the baby at first. But when I went home and took my father aside, I told him you'd be arriving at the house and that he and my mother were going to be grandparents. He didn't take it well. He threatened to disown me. He wasn't even going to finish paying for my college education. He said we wouldn't get a dime from him. Nor would I be allowed to run the family business if I didn't get rid of the baby."

Jewel didn't have any sympathy for him, just because his father was some kind of sub-human form. "You turned your back on me when I needed you most. Wouldn't even let me inside your parents' home. Do you know how low I felt that day — that whole week?"

Rightfully, shame etched across Barrington's face. "I was young, we both were young. I was terrified of my father back then." Barrington turned to Jackson. "Brent feels the same way I did at his age. But if he had someone like you to take him under his wing. He'd probably be a better man for it."

Jewel put a hand on Jackson's, trying to show support for him. If he wanted Brent as a client, she didn't want to get in the way. Having a man like Jackson around might help Brent to become a better man than his brother. "I already told Jackson that I think he's the perfect agent for Brent. I don't want your brother to suffer just because he has an evil brother."

"I deserve that. I didn't treat you kindly. But I'm not the same man I was back then, and I truly am sorry for what I did to you."

Jewel wasn't interested in apologies. Could he get her baby back? Could he take away the years she spent hiding her shame from her family? But she had to know, so she asked, "So when did you finally grow up enough to realize what you did to me was wrong?"

"I'm not proud of how long it took. But it was when I met my wife. She'd had a similar experience, and it tormented her. I promised her that she had nothing to fear from me. But every day after that, I was reminded of what I did to you. Then when she told me she was pregnant, I thought that maybe I could make amends for not doing the right thing with my first baby by becoming the kind of dad my baby will need. I doubt if I'll be perfect, but I've been praying."

15

Praying — he said he's been praying. A man like Barrington was able to pray to God while Jewel hadn't felt qualified to go to God since she made the worst decision of her life. The knowledge of that burned deep in her soul. Barrington had been horrible to her. Treated her like she was nothing. But God had granted him another chance to do the right thing. He now had a wife and a child on the way.

But at thirty-two, Jewel still wasn't married and didn't have a child. Unless she counted her child that was in heaven. She wasn't like those who sought to make abortion less weighty by convincing oneself that the baby wasn't human unless the woman wanted to give birth. A fetus, was a baby, was a human, plain and simple.

Now the baby she selfishly destroyed lived in heaven while she remained tormented on earth. Jewel kicked a rock that had rolled in from the sea as she walked the beach. She'd gotten away from everyone and just started walking and talking to God. She needed answers, and only God could give her what she sought. So, whether He chose to ignore her or not, she was coming for Him like Jacob when he wrestled with an angel and said, 'I'm not going to let you go until you bless me'.

But more than a blessing, Jewel needed forgiveness. Tears streamed down her face as she completely blocked out any of the people passing by. This was between her and God. Once and for all, she had to know if she too could be forgiven.

She was looking out at the sea, but Jewel wasn't thinking of floating away with her sins. No, this time, she wanted to cast her cares and believe that God would catch and drop them so deep that they never rose up against her again.

Her mind traveled back to the words of her mother, 'If God can forget and forgive your sins, why can't you?'

All these years, Jewel thought it had been God denying her the forgiveness she craved because He just didn't love her anymore. But had she actually been in her own way? Had she stepped in the place of God and condemned her own self as unworthy to the point that she hadn't noticed whether God had forgiven her or not?

She looked toward heaven. "I loved You so much when I was younger. Always wanted to do the right thing for You. But I lost my way, and that separated me from You. I don't want to be apart from You anymore. Can you ever forgive me?"

The wind blew against her sundress and seemed to sway her closer to the water. She felt compelled to move forward. Just let the sea water cleanse her. "Set me free, Lord."

The hot heat of the sun beat down on her head as the cold, cool refreshing water washed over her feet. The water welcomed her, invited her to come a little further. "Is that You, Lord? Should I keep going?"

Come to Me all who labor and are heavy laden, and I will give you rest.

Did she just hear God, or was she remembering a Bible verse that she'd read during youth church? Whatever this was, it felt real to her, like God was calling her home. Back to the place where she had once been with him. She kept putting one foot in front of the other, walking into the sea. She stretched out her arms. Reaching… reaching until she sank deep into the water.

The water rocked her back and forth as one wave after another slammed against her body. She went under. Jewel started flapping her arms, she was drowning. She had to get her head above water. As the current kept trying to take her under, Jewel found herself calling on the name of Jesus.

"Jesus!" Yes, He was her savior. He had always been there for her, even when she didn't want to know Him. Didn't want to be judged by Him. But now, she needed Him. Had always needed Him. And would forever need the Lord in her life.

"Forgive me, Lord," she screamed as her head lifted above the water. The current pushed her toward land. As Jewel laid on the sand, not caring if another current overtook her and rushed her back out to sea because, in that water, she felt renewed, refreshed, reborn even. This time it had happened. God heard her plea — and God had forgiven.

As she sat up on her knees, looked heavenward, Jewel was now and forevermore, ready to finally and completely forgive herself. "Thank You, Lord. Thank You for loving me, even when I sinned against You."

She got off the ground, dusted some of the sand from her arms and legs, then ran down the beach toward her mother's villa. She had to share this experience with her Mom before anyone else. The woman who'd been praying for her for so long, should be the first to know that God answered her prayers.

"Mom, are you here?" She beat on the front door. It wasn't five o'clock yet. So, they shouldn't be at rehearsal. "Mama." She banged against the door again.

"Hold on child, don't knock the door down." Vanetta opened the door and stared at her daughter. "Bradley, bring one of them beach towels," she yelled over her shoulder. She then turned back to Jewel. "What happened to you? You're soaking wet and look at all the sand and water dripping from your dress."

Bradley was walking toward Vanetta with a towel in hand.

Throwing up her hands, her face glowing. "I've been baptized, Mama. God has set me free."

"Oh, my Lord." Vanetta wrapped her arms around her daughter and hugged her so tight that she was now wet and dripping with sand and water.

Bradley turned back toward the patio. "I'll get another beach towel." He grabbed it. And then helped both women towel off. Then he suggested, "I think we should take this out to the back patio. No sense giving this resort any reason to charge us extra fees."

Vanetta giggled. "Your father's right. Let's go to the patio. I want to hear all about this."

"But Mama, it's almost time for the rehearsal. I need to get changed so we won't be late." Jewel had been late or a no-show at so many events that were planned for her parents that she didn't want to miss not one more thing.

But Vanetta shushed her concerns. "If you don't get in here and tell me and your dad what the Lord has done for you — we don't care nothing about being a little late for that rehearsal. Like your dad keeps reminding me, we are already married, and that isn't going to be undone."

"Praise Jesus," Bradley said as he ushered Jewel to the patio.

They sat down, Jewel wrapped the towel around herself. Excitement ran through her body like fireworks on the Fourth of July. "I was walking on the beach. At first, I was downing myself because Barrington was able to pray, and I hadn't felt qualified to go to God in a very long time. I started crying and asking God to please forgive me."

Bradley was seated next to Vanetta. He took his wife's hand in his and squeezed it. A tear rolled down Vanetta's face. Bradley wiped it away. "No more tears, hon. It's time to rejoice."

"That's how I feel too, Daddy." Jewel hugged him. "I heard God telling me to come to Him, so I went out into the water. I thought I was going to drown when the current swept me away, but instead, I came out of the water feeling refreshed and reborn. God has forgiven me."

~~~

With so much excitement going on, the Dawson family still managed to make it to the wedding rehearsal and the rehearsal dinner. Since they had planned to allow their parents to spend the last two nights on the resort as their honeymoon, they all brought their presents to the reception dinner.

Since they were on the beach and seafood was readily available, the reception dinner was all about lobster, crab legs, and shrimp. Delicious, delectable, and delightful were the words Jewel would have used to describe the evening. She especially loved it when her grandparents toasted her parents. They saluted Bradley and Vanetta with words of love and admiration that brought tears to everyone's eyes.

When it was time for the gifts, Jewel clapped and laughed her head off as her parents opened Serena's gift. It was sexy attire for both of them.

Serena stood as her mother shot her a questioning glance. "Y'all always embarrassing me with your, how-you-think-you-go-here comments, so I decided to let y'all have at it this weekend."

Bradley quickly put the lingerie back in the box. "Thank you, daughter. We will return the favor when you get married."

"No, Daddy, don't do that. I won't be able to take it." Kayla shouted as she giggled hysterically.

Pop-Pop and Grandma Priscilla gave the couple a portrait they had painted of them.

"It's beautiful." Vanetta hugged her mother-in-love and father-in-love. "You two have been so good to me. I thank God that I was blessed with in-laws like you."

Grandma Priscilla wagged her finger. "After all these years, we're just mom and dad, no in-law nothing."

Jewel loved that her grandmother had said that. Her mother had lost both her parents fifteen years ago, and it was Priscilla who had helped her heal from that devastation.

Jewel handed her gift to her parents, which was more of an envelope. "Honestly, I couldn't think of anything you two needed, because you seem so happy with what you've acquired over the years. So, I wasn't going to try to replace any portraits in the house or anything." Jewel shrugged. "Maybe if I had thought like my grandparents and had a painting done of the two of you, that would have been something."

"Oh, stop," her dad told her. "Whatever you got us is just fine." He opened the envelope, and a broad smile crossed his face. "Good looking out," he told his daughter as he showed his wife the contents of the envelope.

"Not you too, Jewel." Vanetta shook her head at the antics of her children.

"Hey, you start your official honeymoon after the ceremony in the morning. Why not get a couples massage."

Serena high-fived Jewel as she laughed. "Don't y'all come back from this trip with another baby. I can tell you now, I'm not babysitting."

"Shut-up, Serena." Face turning red, Vanetta tried turned away from the group.

Jewel pointed at her. "I can't believe, after all the stuff you say to us about the marriage bed being one of God's great gifts to marriages, that you are actually blushing."

"Oh, you got your day coming, Jewel. So, you and Jackson just get ready," Vanetta said, trying to keep the grin off her face.

Jackson puffed up his chest. "Bring it on, we ain't scared."

Jewel pushed him back into his seat. "Don't encourage them. You don't know them like I do."

Kayla handed her gift to her parents. "In keeping with the mantra, Dad just said that anything we get is fine. I hope you like what I got y'all because it was from the heart and all I could afford."

They opened the gift and held up two t-shirts. One said I'm His Forever, and the other said, I'm Hers Forever. The group exploded with "Awwww."

Vanetta and Bradley then stood to thank everyone. "This has been the most beautiful time of our lives." Vanetta held her hand to her heart as a tear escaped her soft brown eyes. "We didn't get everything right in all these years of being married and being parents to you beautiful young women. But I hope y'all know that we did our best, and after all these years, we're still standing." She glanced at Jewel, "And with the help of the good Lord, we're getting better each and every day. So, we truly have a lot to celebrate and be thankful for."

Bradley cut in. "Thank you all for making this week so very special." He held onto Vanetta's hand tightly. "Since the day I met this beautiful woman, I always just wanted to see her smile. It broke my heart to tell her we couldn't have a twenty-fifth vow renewal ceremony. I never knew how I would make that up to her, but I kept praying." He lifted his free hand up, shook it as if praising. He was then overcome with emotion and tears filled his eyes. "God's word says that a good man leaves an inheritance for his children, so I just couldn't take care of the things we wanted without making sure you girls had what y'all needed."

Serena wiped the tears from her face. "You took care of us, Daddy. We are so grateful for having parents like you and mom."

Bradley shook his head, not willing to take any praise. "I was just doing what the Bible said a good man should do for his kids. But the blessed part about it is how y'all turned around and blessed us. Y'all had no knowledge of the thing I desired to give to my wife — each time I bought your mom flowers, it was a way of apologizing for coming up short."

Jewel loved her daddy. He was the kind of man other men should aspire to become. "We might not have known the desires of your hearts, but God knew, Daddy, God always knows."

"That's right, my Jewel, God always knows," he agreed. "Well, anyway, I just wanted to say I'm thankful."

Bradley and Vanetta were about to sit down when Jackson jumped up. "You've got one last present to open."

"Jackson." Vanetta's mouth just about hung open. "You already snuck in and covered the fee for our trip. You can't keep spoiling us. You and Jewel need money to live on, so don't spend it all on the family, you hear me?"

Jackson nodded. "I promise I will be wise with my money. This is the last gift until your next anniversary or Christmas, how 'bout that?"

"Wiseguy, huh?" Bradley received the small package from Jackson and then handed it to Vanetta. "You're his favorite, so you might as well open it."

"Daddy, Jackson doesn't have any favorites between you two," Jewel admonished.

But Jackson shook his head. "No. No, he's right. Mama Vanetta has a special place in my heart. But your daddy still makes me call him Mr. Dawson."

The group laughed.

Vanetta untied the ribbon and tore the wrapping paper off the small package. There were two membership cards inside. In stunned silence, she handed the box to Bradley.

Bradley's eyes misted over again. He pulled Jackson to him and hugged the man. "Don't you ever call me Mr. again. From now on, I'm Dad or Papa Dawson, whatever you're comfortable with, Son. You hear me?"

Grinning like he'd finally won the Olympic gold medal he'd trained all his life for, Jackson said, "Yes sir — I mean, Dad… Papa Dawson." He shook his head. "We'll figure it out."

When Jackson sat back down, Jewel leaned in and asked, "What is he so excited about?"

"I got him and your mom a one-year membership to that country club he enjoyed so much. Now, I don't have to take them, they can go whenever they want."

"Jackson, you are a really, really good man. I love you for how thoughtful you are." They kissed. Jewel usually loved pressing her lips to Jackson's, but she got this uneasy feeling about it. She knew what was bothering her. She hadn't told Jackson about the experience she had on the beach yet. She would have to tell him soon because life was going to be different from now on. No more just showing up to church on Mother's day or Resurrection Sunday. Jewel wanted a real relationship with the God who had forgiven all her transgressions.

God had changed her. She wasn't the same old Jewel anymore. She was beginning to think differently, see things differently. She only prayed that Jackson could find a way to let God into his heart as well. Because just like the t-shirt Kayla purchased for her parents said, she wanted to be his forever, and she wanted him to be her forever. But now she knew that could only be possible if she and Jackson do what her parents and grandparents had done — let God lead them.

16

As Jewel walked out to the beach where the wedding would take place, with Jackson beside her, she wore the peach colored dress her mom had picked out. And Jackson wore the grey suit her dad had picked out. She noticed that the arch had been placed just ten feet from where she'd gone into the water and had her rebirth experience with God. She looked to heaven, "You always, know, don't You, Lord?"

"You say something?"

Jewel's eyes were on the sea and the heavens. "I was talking to God. Don't you think it's amazing how He knows how things will turn out, but we're all just here walking it out day by day."

Jackson shrugged. "I guess."

Jewel was still musing about the infinite wisdom of her Savior. "If you would have told me last week that my mother and father would have full knowledge of what I did back in college, I would have stayed home, climbed under the covers, and barely peeked my head out for the shame that would be revealed."

She twirled in the sand then came back to her love. "But God knows what's best. He set me up this week, and then He set me free."

His eyebrows furrowed. "I don't get it Jewel, set you free? We are all free. Nobody owns us."

Serena and Kayla ran up behind them. They looked so beautiful in their peach dresses. Because it was a beach wedding, they each wore just above the knee, strapless dresses. But their grandmother, who was making her way toward them, wore a long dress with short sleeves. She was, after all, the maid-of-honor, so her dress could be a little different.

"Y'all look so beautiful."

"You are quite beautiful yourself, Jewel." Kayla glanced over at Jackson. "And the best future brother-in-law in the world is looking good too."

He smiled. "Thanks, Kayla. At least I'm appreciated by one of the Dawson sisters."

Jewel shoved him. "Stop it. You know I love you."

"Yeah." He nodded. "But it's nice to hear sometimes."

"Okay, you lollygaggers, let's get to this wedding." Grandma Priscilla ushered them forward.

Daddy was waiting with the minister, and Pop-Pop was standing beside him. The music started. It was instrumental, but even without words, it sounded like love, joy, and an I-just-wanna-be-with-you, kind of melody.

The girls and Jackson weren't going to walk down the aisle since there weren't equal men and women for both sides. White wooden chairs had been set out for them. Serena and Kayla sat on one side of the aisle, and Jewel and Jackson sat on the other side as they watched Vanetta Dawson walked down the aisle for the wedding she'd never had.

Her mother was beautiful in a cream colored dress that was form-fitting at the top to the waist. Then beads danced around her waist just as the dress swayed all the way to the floor. It was understated perfection at its best. Even the bouquet was perfect.

Filled with multi-colored flowers, it draped down to the point where her dress flowed outward.

She walked down the aisle by herself, but when the minister asked, "Who gives this woman to be married?"

Pop-Pop stepped forward and took her arm. "I do, with pleasure." His words echoed in the wind. He then placed a soft, gentle kiss on her mother's cheek as he ushered her forward.

Now standing in front of Dad where she was always meant to be, Jewel and her sisters watched as their mother married their father — again.

Jewel and Jackson rented another cabana and lounged around the rest of the afternoon, basking in the sun and the glory of the day.

"I loved everything about that wedding. Do you think we should consider a beach wedding?"

"Nah," Jewel shook her head. "I loved it for my mother and father. But they've been married for a long time and have already solidified their walk with God. I want to be married in a church. Matter-of-fact, I'm going to join my parents' church when we get back home."

"Hold on." Jackson sat up. "We never talked about joining some church. I'm not sure I'm ready for that."

"Jackson, it only makes sense. We're both in our thirties, it's time for us to get serious about other things besides our career."

"Other things like what?"

"Like God, church, and even children. I think it would be wonderful to have three or four children that look like you." She touched his caramel face. Joy was in her eyes today. She wanted to feel this way always.

"Pump your breaks." Jackson wasn't feeling it. "I was thinking about one or two. I don't know where you're getting three or four kids from. When I first brought up the issues of kids, you didn't even want to talk about having one, now you want four."

"Jackson, you know what I was dealing with. I couldn't think about more kids when I hadn't forgiven myself for what I'd done to my first child." She sat up and faced him. "But God has forgiven me, and I have forgiven me too. So, I want to live and try to be happy and enjoy what's left. If you don't want four kids. I'm good with two, but we have to have at least have two."

He nodded. "I think we can compromise on that. Two or three will be fine, but they have to look like their beautiful mother." He jabbed his cheek. "I don't want them with this mug."

"That's a very handsome mug you've got there." They kissed.

But as they pulled back, Jackson said, "What's up with you and church all of a sudden. First, your dad hits me with this 'a man must love his wife like Christ loves the church' stuff." He did his best imitation of Bradley Dawson. "Now you're all God this and church that. I'm just not with it."

"Let me ask you something, Jackson. Your father has been married four times."

"Right. True that. Poppa was a rolling stone and all that."

"Did he allow God to be the center in any of his marriages?"

Again, Jackson was stuck with furrowed brows; he just didn't get it. "Not sure what you mean by 'center', but as far as I know, my dad has never been a churchgoer."

Jewel looked around, searching for some way to explain what she knew they needed. A volleyball net was set up not far from where they lounged. "Come with me." She jogged down the beach.

"Where are we going?" Putting on his shoes and following, he yelled, "Don't go too far, I don't want to lose our cabana."

She stopped next to the volleyball net. As he came closer, she put her hand on the cord that had been wrapped around the poll, which helped the net stay up. "What do you see?"

He shrugged. "A cord."

She nodded like the lesson was going well. "Yes, but look a little closer, how many cords have been wrapped around each other to make this one cord."

It only took him a second to look at the cord and answer, "Three."

"Without this cord, the net wouldn't work, would it? It wouldn't affix to the poll correctly and the net wouldn't be complete."

He nodded again.

"And why do you think three smaller cords were tied together to make this one cord that's holding this net to the poll?"

"Because it's somehow stronger with three cords than just one or two."

"Exactly. And the Bible tells us that a threefold cord is not easily broken." With her fingers, she touched each smaller cord as she said, "God. The Holy Spirit. Jesus." She went back over the cords again, but this time said, "Man. Woman. God."

Jackson didn't say anything. Just stared at her.

"Don't you get it, Jackson? I believe that it's the third cord that helps a marriage stand the test of time. If we allow God to be the head of our household, then you and I will be able to make it through anything. And that's what I want, so yes, I want to go to church."

She thought surely he would agree. She wasn't asking for a kidney, just a commitment to get serious about God because she believed that would help them stay together.

"Sooo, no prenup, but church on Sunday."

"And Wednesday. My mother's church has Bible study on Wednesday night. I used to love Bible study when I was younger. It's about time I got back to it."

"Do you hear yourself?" They started walking back to the cabana. "You're talking about the things that you love, but you're not taking into consideration what I want — I golf on Sunday mornings."

Nobody was more confused than Jewel right about now. Jackson had traveled all the way to Antigua, paid for her entire family to stay in a fabulous resort, and cancelled a deal that could have made him millions all because he loved her, but he couldn't commit to going to church even though he knew she needed that from him?

"Okay, we compromised on the number of kids. Let's strike another compromise. No prenup, and you can go to church as much as you want. And I'll sleep in or golf." He smiled at her like he'd solved the problem. "That's good, right?"

Without knowing or understanding, Jackson had just broken her heart. Jewel had given her life back to God, she felt such peace — a peace that she hadn't felt in a long time. She wasn't going to throw that away, not even for Jackson.

If she knew anything, it was like-minded people had the best chance at a long-lasting marriage. What if Jackson had an event on Sunday and demanded that she go with him rather than attend church? Would they grow to hate each other because of the differences that now divide them? She lovingly put her hand on Jackson's oh so gorgeous face. "My Baby-Boo, you were everything I wanted — until I discovered what I truly need."

"What's that suppose to mean?"

Sorrow filled her eyes. She knew that Jackson loved her. She loved him, but she also loved God and would never ever compromise that relationship again. Not knowing how much it had cost her when she had chosen her will — to date Barrington rather than God's will for her to wait for the man He predestined to find her.

They stood, she hugged him so tight, trying to draw in his manly scent, imprint it on her heart, so she'd never forget what this kind of love felt like, smelled like, tasted like. She kissed him, then pulled away as she took the engagement ring off her finger one last time. "I'm sorry, but I can't marry you."

17

Jackson would have kept fighting for Jewel if he thought it would do any good. But what mere man could fight God and win. Her mind was made up, she'd had some kind of spiritual awakening, and that was that. He was a man who had loved and lost. Selah.

Back home, Jackson got to work. The 2019 draft was in less than thirty days and he had a few prospects like Aubrey and Brent to get into as many workouts as possible. Other agents may have the number one and two picks, but he had some guys that would stand the test of time in this business, and when it was all over, Jackson was confident that Aubrey and Brent would become not just All-Stars, but Hall of Fame players.

Jackson was glad that Jewel had given him the green light to work with Brent, but he'd told his young client that he wouldn't take orders from his father. If he was going to represent Brent, then he would only take his marching orders from Brent himself. If they didn't like it, then they could fire him and get another agent.

"I'm cool with it," Brent told him. "My dad has done a lot to get my skills up. But I'm a man now. And I need to be making my own decisions."

Busying himself with work, Jackson tried not to think about Jewel and her love affair with Jesus. What was that about anyway?

He was so puzzled about the whole thing that his mind wouldn't let it go. Couldn't let it go.

He had so many questions, like how could she refuse to marry him just because they didn't agree about religion? Who does that? Maybe, she really never loved him in the first place. She'd been trying to get out of marrying him ever since he gave her that prenup.

Maybe it had been all about the money. But he'd taken the prenup off the table and Jewel still gave back his ring. So, maybe it was just like she said. It was a God thing and he didn't measure up. Just let it go.

But even as he tried to get Jewel off his mind, his housekeeper rushed toward him carrying Jewel's charm bracelet. "I found Ms. Jewel's charm bracelet. Please tell her it was in between the sofa cushions. I turned everything over to find it for her."

Holding the bracelet in his hand like it had diamonds and rubies on it rather than a cross, heart, open Bible, and a high heel shoe. "Jewel called here? When?"

The woman shook her head. "No, sir, she called my cell a few days ago, but I didn't have you on my schedule until today."

"Why didn't you call me, I could have looked for it?" He didn't like how irritated he sounded, because his housekeeper was one of the nicest women he'd ever had the pleasure of knowing. He would have loved having her for a grandmother.

"Ms. Jewel told me not to bother you." She patted his hand that held the bracelet. "But you get it to her, okay. A girls got to have her bracelet."

Yeah, a girls got to have her bracelet, but not the man who bought her the heart charm on the bracelet. Jewel's mother had purchased the bracelet and bought her the cross and the open Bible. Jewel had purchased the shoe charm herself, and since he knew how much she loved that bracelet, he'd gotten her the heart on their three month anniversary. Shaking his head, he told himself, "Get to work."

Jackson headed over to the Spectrum Arena, where Aubrey was doing a workout. He seriously doubted that Aubrey would fall low enough in the draft for the Hornets to have a chance at him. But Aubrey and his father had attended so many games at the Spectrum arena when Aubrey was coming up, and they'd talk about how one day Aubrey would one day play ball for Charlotte.

John was courtside chopping it up with the Hornet announcers, who also happened to be former ballers. Jackson and John clasped hands.

"You covering this for ESPN? Cause if so, make sure the cameraman gets a few takes of my man, Aubrey, while he's out there showing out."

John shook his head. "Nah, man, had to get out the house."

"That bad?"

"Do you remember how ticked I was with Green when he elbowed me in the neck and shoved me down so hard on the court that I hurt my back and eventually ended my basketball career?"

How could he forget? John had been having his best year and had just signed his biggest contract. He was headed to the All-Stars again for sure. Then in a game that didn't matter to either team, John had been injured. Within two years, he was out of the league.

"Well, I wouldn't wish what I'm going through on that guy."

"You're the one who tried to turn a stripper into a housewife."

John looked like a man who gambled and lost. "I know, right."

The cloud of sadness around John was too much for Jackson to deal with at the moment. He wanted to be a friend and provide sympathy. But he wasn't about to win any best friend award today, because he had no sympathy — had no words. He needed space and distance because if he stood next to John a second longer, he'd probably start crying and make a fool of himself in front of men he had to work with. So, he searched around for someplace else to stand.

Aubrey's dad sat in the bleachers watching his boy. Jackson climbed the bleachers, John stopped him. "Hey man, that was foul how they played Scottie."

"Tell me about it." Jackson hadn't even received a courtesy call. The Panthers had cut Scottie after he'd had his best year in the NFL. But Jackson wasn't worried. A talent like Scottie wouldn't stay a free agent for long.

Jackson turned back toward Aubrey's dad and continued up the bleachers to get to row Q. "You can come down to the courtside seats and watch if you want, Pastor Walton. You don't have to sit up here."

But Pastor Walton shook his head, smiled as he patted the seat next to him. "Me and my boy used to sit right here and watch the games. You see, I make a good, but not a great living as a pastor. I can't afford private jets or courtside seats. But these seats right here made me a hero to my boy."

"Pretty soon, your boy will be able to buy you any seat you want in whichever arena he plays in." As soon as he said it, Jackson knew it was the wrong thing to say. He didn't want Pastor Walton thinking that what he had been able to afford was somehow less than what Aubrey will soon be able to afford. "You know what, strike that. Because I don't think it's about the seats in the arena at all, is it?"

"Nope." Pastor Walton kept his eye on Aubrey as he ran drills. "I just want him to be happy and to always remember that he rode on the coattails of a lot of prayers. God has brought him this far, and he will take Aubrey even higher if he can find a way to never forget his first love."

Jackson sat down next to Pastor Walton. "I can see why my ex-fiancé's family attends your church. Y'all alike."

"Ex? I didn't even know the two of you had gotten engaged. When did all this happen?"

"It was kinda over before it started. We got engaged two weeks ago, but we just couldn't see eye to eye on something, so."

"Sorry to hear that. But, just so you know, Jewel joined our church this past Sunday, and we are thrilled to have her."

Jackson nodded. Then he turned to the Pastor and asked, "Do you really think it's a big deal if a wife goes to church while her husband stays home or goes golfing?" He shrugged after saying it like he already knew he was wrong for wanting to golf rather than go to church.

Pastor Walton gave him a tired-of-answering-this-question look. "Let me turn that around and ask you a question."

Jackson adjusted in his seat, already knowing this conversation wasn't going to go the way he wanted it to.

"If someone came into your office, offered to partner with you and share half the office and costs associated with bringing in clients for half the proceeds, but then he told you that he knew nothing about sports and had no interest in learning, what would you say to an offer like that?"

"I'd tell him to get them jokes outta my face."

"And why would you think he wasn't serious about partnering with you?"

"Because he had no love for the game. How can you be in this business without a love for the game?"

Pastor Walton nodded as if Jackson had answered his own question. "Kind of like the question the Bible asks… 'how can two walk together unless they agree'. You see, a woman who loves God knows she's fighting a losing battle trying to have a relationship with a man who doesn't also love God because the two will never agree."

"But Jewel and I weren't like that. We have a lot in common. She likes sports. We both love seafood. We're both competitive, but can also be happy spending a quiet day together. Jewel was made for me, Pastor. I just don't know how to get her to see that. I mean, how can I fight against God?"

"Instead of fighting, have you thought about joining her?"

Jackson shrugged. "I guess I just don't get the hype, Pastor." He held up a hand, trying to qualify his statement before it was taken way out of context. "I believe in God. And after spending last week with the Dawson family, I can even appreciate His goodness. But I sleep in on Sundays." And when he wasn't sleeping in, he was at a football or basketball game or playing golf. Jackson doubted that God appreciated any of the things he enjoyed.

Pastor Walton laughed. "I remember saying that myself. Even told God about my golf game and how much networking I did on the course. But God has a way of getting our attention." He put a hand on Jackson's shoulder. "My wife prayed me in. So watch out young man, because if Jewel is praying for you, you might as well buy some Sunday suits because you will be at church."

~~~

On Thursday evening, the Dawson sisters met up at their parents' house for an evening of board games and a movie. Jewel was still a bit down about the breakup, but she'd joined the church on Sunday and had been reading her Bible every day, so she was making it.

"You are taking this break up better than I would have expected, based on how Kayla and I found you the last time you gave back the ring," Serena told her sister.

"I've cried a few times, but God is helping me get through this. Like pastor said, faith plus patience equals the promise. So, I'm going to wait patiently to see what God has for me."

Vanetta's lip turned upside down. "But have you talked to him."

"No, Mother, and I don't want you calling him interfering in my business this time."

Trying to lighten the mood, Kayla asked, "Have you been doing drive-bys. You know how we do it. Act like we ain't thinking about the guy, but all the while tracking him like we on the FBI payroll."

Jewel rolled her eyes. "No, Kayla. I haven't turned into a stocker." But it wasn't like she hadn't thought about it. She had misplaced her charm bracelet and had wanted to go to Jackson's to look for it, and admittedly, to see Jackson's handsome face one more time. But she couldn't do that. So, she contacted his housekeeper. Gloria would contact her soon enough to let her know if her bracelet was at Jackson's place. If it wasn't there, she had no clue where else it could be.

Her dad had been standing in the doorway between the living room and the hallway. He stared at them like he wanted to knock some heads together. "Okay, while y'all talking about calling, visiting, and stalking, has anybody prayed for the boy?"

Jewel got up from her spot on the floor, walked over to her dad, and kissed him on the cheek. "You try to act all hard, but you like Jackson."

"Hey, he did give me and your mom memberships to that country club."

Jewel frowned at her father. "It shouldn't be about gifts, Dad. Either you like him, or you don't."

"I'm just joking, Jewel. I'll give back those memberships if you want me to. Marriage is hard enough, but if you get in it with someone who doesn't have the same convictions as you and doesn't value the things that you value, it will become the biggest struggle of your life."

Vanetta picked up one of the pillows off the sofa and threw it at her husband. "What's this about marriage being hard."

Bradley put a hand to his heart. "Not our marriage, sweet Netta. You and I have grown together because we made up our minds to put God first early in our marriage. I just think we need to be praying for Jackson. So, that he too can realize what's most important."

Vanetta stood next to Bradley. They held hands. "Your father is right. Let's pray for Jackson."

The Dawson family came together, bowed their heads before a holy God, and prayed for Jackson Lewis like he'd never been prayed for before.

18

Getting off his flight and heading home on a Saturday night, Jackson was finally feeling as if he could work without thinking about the situation with Jewel every other minute. He was now at about the five-minute mark, yes, he could go five minutes without feeling like his heart wanted to just give up and give out.

But at least he was able to do something special for Brent today. Brent had a workout with the Miami Heat, and he killed it. The coach promised that we'd be hearing from him, and Jackson was able to get Brent a workout with another team out West for Sunday evening. He was going home to get some sleep before getting right back on the plane in the morning to head to Portland.

In the cab ride home, Jackson pulled out his cell and began scrolling through some of the pictures he and Jewel took in Antigua. They had such a good time on that island. Jewel dealt with her past, and Jackson really thought that his presence helped her as she relived those horrible, awful, no-good days of her past. But it hadn't been him at all; evidently, God was all she needed.

He still had her bracelet and knew that she would love to have it back. The bracelet was special to her, even if he wasn't anymore.

He touched Jewel's name in his call log, but stopped. He took a deep breath. "You can do this." Just as his heart was about to give up again, he touched Jewel's name in his call log and let it ring.

She answered on the third ring. She used to answer his calls on the first ring. Guess he wasn't that important anymore. "Hey, are you busy? What are you doing?"

"No, just ironing."

"Ironing? What are you ironing?" He knew it was small talk, but that was all he had left.

"An outfit that I need for church tomorrow."

She was going to church. He should have known. This was the difference in their lives. Jewel was now going to church on Sundays, and he was getting back on a plane heading out West tomorrow for business. "Pastor Walton told me you've been attending his church."

"I have. I feel at home there. I love how Pastor Walton ministers the word."

Jackson loved the sound of Jewel's voice. It soothed him. He wanted to lean back, rest his head against the headrest in the cab and let her voice guide him back to the beach where they held hands and got sand in their shoes.

"Jackson, are you there?"

He sat back up. So much for daydreaming. "I'm here. Look, I called to tell you that Gloria found your bracelet. I can bring it to you if you'd like."

"Oh, thank God. I turned my apartment upside down looking for it. When I hadn't heard from Gloria, I thought it wasn't at your place either."

"She gave it to me the other day. I'm sorry it took me so long to call."

"You don't have to apologize, Jackson. I know you are extremely busy right now. By the way, how is everything going for Aubrey and Brent?"

Their conversation was pleasant, but Jackson could tell that Jewel was making a concerted effort to keep them on a nothing-personal-level. "Things are going well. I think both of them will do well in the draft next month."

"Good, I'm glad for them and for you, Jackson."

He knew she meant it. Just was sad that she wouldn't be there, sharing the excitement with him. "Hey, so, when's a good time for me to bring your bracelet?"

What could he say? She wasn't going to take kindly to his work schedule getting in the way, especially on a Sunday. But it is what it is. "I have to fly back out in the morning. Can I bring it to you on Monday evening? Would that work?"

"Yes, of course, that's fine."

That's what her mouth said, but Jackson heard the disappointment in her voice. He hated that he'd disappointed her once again. Maybe Jewel was right, they didn't belong together. "Talk to you soon, Jewel. Oh, and enjoy yourself at church tomorrow."

"I will, Jackson. Be safe on your flight out in the morning. I'll be praying for you."

That was a new one. She'd never offered to pray for him before. And Jackson hadn't thought much about needing prayer since life had been going good for him. But if she could pray away this all consuming feeling of loss, he'd appreciate it. "Thanks, Jewel. I think I'd like prayer."

They hung up just as the cabbie pulled up to his condo. Lights were on in the living room, which Jackson thought strange because he always turned all of his lights off whenever he left the house. Something his mama taught him.

Only two people had a key to his condo. He'd just gotten off the phone with Jewel. She was at her place ironing so that only left one other person. Rolling his eyes heavenward, he prepared himself for the drama he was about to experience.

He opened the door and sat his briefcase down. "Dad? Are you in here?"

Jack strolled into the living room from the back of the house. He looked like he'd wrestled with a mighty wind and lost. "Hey, Son. I didn't think you'd be back tonight."

Jackson cocked his head at that. "So, why are you here, then?"

"You know how it goes." Jack sucked his teeth. "These women — can't live with 'em… can't live without 'em."

Heading into the kitchen to get a bottle of water, Jackson dismissed his father's foolishness. "Why do you even bother to get married? Why don't you just meet a woman and then break-up with her? That would save you a lot of time and money, don't you think?"

"What can I say, Son. I'm just in love with the idea of love, I guess." Jack plopped down on the sofa, put his feet up on the coffee table, turned on the television, and started scrolling through channels.

Jackson wasn't having it. Not this time. "You can't stay here."

"Come on, Son, don't be like that. This thing with Vivian will blow over in a couple of days, then I'll go back home. You're not going to be home much anyway because you're working on the draft."

"I'm glad you know my schedule. But whether I'm home or not, you're not going to be here. Go home and make things right with Vivian before you end up on search number five."

Jack shook his head. Vivian's impossible to deal with. Just let me sleep on the couch a few nights. You won't even know I'm here."

Jackson sat down in the chair across from his Dad. He loved the old fart, but the man had taught him wrong about so many things. Now he was about to give his father a life lesson he learned from a man who knew exactly what it took to make a woman happy. "A wise man once told me that kicking a man out of his bedroom was like taking a king off his throne. So, you got one question to answer, do you want to be the king of your house, or do you want to keep going from house to house, wife to wife? When does it end, Dad?"

Jack wasn't quite getting it. "But sometimes a woman needs time to cool off."

"Y'all cool off together." He leaned forward, really trying to break this down the way Jewel's dad and granddad had broken it down to him. "See, marriage isn't supposed to be sweet and sunshine every day you wake up. You and Vivian are going to have good days, and then you're going to have really bad days.

"But those are the days you'll need each other the most. Those are the days that you pray for your wife and maybe tell her that you're sorry for being a jerk." Had he really just told his dad to pray for his wife? It sounds so simple, almost too simple when the Dawson men explained it to him. Jackson had been throwing money at his problem and never once thought to pray about what he and Jewel were dealing with. He didn't know how well something like that could work for his dad either, but it was worth a try.

Jack smiled at that. "My mama used to tell me to pray until something happens. One time I didn't get this promotion that I just knew was mine. I told her about it. She said, "Did you pray about it?"

"I admitted that I hadn't prayed. And your grandma took the palm of her hand a swatted me a good one on the back of my head.

In a voice like he was mimicking his mama, Jack said, "If you stop praying before your change comes, it's your fault, not Gods."

"Wow, you never told me that before. Sounds like Grandma Lillian had some wisdom."

"She did. I just wished I had listened to her more. But now she's gone and I've made a mess of my life."

"It's not too late for you, Dad. You just gotta stop running away from your problems and wait for your change to come, like Grandma Lillian said."

Jack was silent. Then he got this thoughtful expression on his face. Picking up the remote again, he channeled surf until he came to a Christian channel. A preacher was behind the podium.

"Since when do you watch the Christian channel?"

"Since my son told me to stop running from my problem. Now be quiet and sit here with your old man for a minute. Let me get a little inspiration in my life."

Jackson was in too much of a state of shock to move. So, he did as his father requested. He thought he was helping his father by sitting there with him so the man could get some inspiration in his life. But as the preacher put his hand firmly on the pulpit, looked directly at the camera as if he was looking directly at him. Jackson began to wonder if God was trying to get his attention.

The preacher said, "Looks to me like mankind has totally forgotten the purpose and plan God created him for from the beginning. Remember, it's not our will, but His will that is to be done on the earth.

"For what plans does man have that are greater than God's plans? What's on your agenda that's greater than God, the Almighty, the Holy One. The One who put breath in your body."

Jack looked to heaven as the preacher closed his message. "I hear You." He stood. "Guess it's time for me to go home." Jack went to the guest bedroom and grabbed his suitcase.

Jackson walked his father to the door. "You think you and Vivian can make it last?"

"Honestly, I don't know. But I'm willing to give it a try... a serious try."

For the first time, in a long time, Jackson was proud of his father. "Never too late to grow up, huh, Dad?" The two men hugged, then Jack left.

As Jackson turned off the lights and headed to his bedroom to get some sleep, his mind kept replaying what the pastor said about a man's plans not being greater than God's plans. He knew that he'd been living by his own agenda all of his life. Only now had he ever stopped to ponder if there could actually be another way of living.

As his head hit the pillow, the last thing he found himself wondering was what life would be like if he was living based on God's will rather than his own...

19

The year was 2025, Jackson knew that because of the calendar on the wall. Jackson stood in the kitchen, making a cup of Macha green tea, and putting a splash of lemon in it. Which was strange because Jackson didn't drink tea.

Everything felt strange to him because it seemed to Jackson that he was watching a man who looked, talked, and moved like he did, but he had no control over anything that he was seeing. He was left to watch… he was dreaming, yes, that's it, he must be dreaming.

Jackson took the cup of tea and a blueberry muffin up the spiral staircase. Wow, some big, fancy place. This wasn't about to be one of those scary dreams, Jackson could feel the good vibes, and the house was sweet. He got comfortable and leaned back to watch the show…

"Good morning, my love," Jackson opened the bedroom door and walked into a master suite that rivaled the suite he and Jewel shared in Antigua. The king-sized four poster bed was placed on one side of the massive room, while an alcove area held a sitting room on the left side of the bedroom that had two beautiful chaise lounge chairs that were so comfortable, you could easily fall asleep on them.

Lifting from the bed, stretching, and yawning, Jewel trained her eyes on him. "Good morning to you as well, my love. And I see you come with breakfast in hand."

Jackson placed the muffin and tea on the night table beside the bed. "You had a rough night, so I wanted to let you sleep in."

Jewel glanced at the clock. "Oh, my goodness." Yawning again. "I overslept. I'm surprised that Josh isn't crying his head off by now."

"I warmed up the bottle you had in the fridge and fed him."

Sitting a little straighter in bed, Jewel pulled Jackson to her and kissed him. "Husband, you are truly a godsend."

Jackson felt something way down deep in his body respond. He loved that Jewel loved him. "How about I go wake the munchkin up and get her a bowl of cereal so we can be on time for church this week."

"Ulterior motives!" Jewel took a bite of her muffin as Jackson headed for the door. "You're only doing breakfast, so we don't embarrass you by being late again. Like a woman with two kids shouldn't be given a little leeway when it comes to punctuality."

"Hey, I'm only trying to help." Then in a tone that sounded like her father was talking to her mother, he added, "So hush that fuss."

He could hear the sound of Jewel's good-natured laughter as he headed down the hallway to wake their little princess. They named her Patricia Netta Lewis. He was sure they'd hear from her once she got old enough to know that her name wasn't in fashion like some of these kids whose names couldn't even be pronounced. But Patricia had been his mother's name, and he loved that a piece of his mother would live on with his daughter.

To keep the peace, Jewel made her middle name Netta, because she said, they'd never live it down if Vanetta Dawson didn't have her name somewhere on her first grandchild. "Wake up, sleepyhead."

"No, Daddy, go away." She pushed his face away as he tried to snuggle noses with her.

"Time to get up, Cia." Cia had been the name they settled on for a little girl with such a grown-up name. "You don't want to be late for children's church, do you?"

"Will they have candy?"

"No candy for you this week. And I don't want you asking for any either, okay?"

"But Daddy, I don't ask for the candy. Whenever I look over at that jar of candy, auntie goes and gets me a piece. Can't help where my eyes go."

He scooped her out of bed. "I'm going to talk to Auntie Kayla about how generous she is with the candy."

"Oh, no, Daddy. Auntie Kayla is much too busy to be talking about candy."

He tickled her as they headed down the stairs. This child was precocious for sure. She looked like him but had her mother's personality in spades, so it was a given that she had him wrapped around her finger. "You let me worry about what Auntie Kayla is too busy for."

He sat her down on one of the stools in front of the kitchen island, then he went into the pantry in search of cereal. He came out holding a box of brand cereal and Frosted Flakes. "Which one?"

Cia put her fist under her chin, stuck her lip out, and pouted. "You know what I want to ask God at children's church today?"

"What?"

"How come, in this whole big house, there's not one box of Fruity Pebbles." Cia slapped her forehead with her open palm, elbow on the counter, looking at her father like how-long-must-I-suffer-with-you.

Jewel walked into the kitchen, took the Frosted Flakes out of his hand, poured some in a bowl with milk, and sat it in front of Cia. "Eat. We don't have all day to fool around with you."

"Thanks." Jackson put the cereal boxes back in the pantry. The little girl had him wrapped. If Jewel hadn't shown up and made Cia eat what was available, he probably would have driven to the store to get those Fruity Pebbles, especially since his child planned to ask God about it.

"The least I can do for the agent who is having such a banner year. First, Aubrey and his team wins the NBA finals, and now Scottie is going to the Super Bowl next Sunday."

Jackson raised his hands in the air and shook them like he was ready to do a happy dance. "Woot, Woot! You can't keep a good man down. I knew I didn't have no scrubs. And look how Scottie got bounced from team to team, and now he's going to the Super Bowl."

"You are the best agent in the business, Baby because it's not just about a paycheck to you. You really believe in these guys." Jewel walked over to the drawer next to the sink, opened it, and pulled out an envelope. She handed the envelope to Jackson with a huge grin on her face. "And now you're going to the Super Bowl!"

"What?" Jackson hurriedly opened the envelope. "Don't play with my emotions."

"I'm not playing. Scottie sent those tickets last night. He said that he understood your stance on attending local games and only out-of-town games once a month. But he figured you'd make an exception for the Super Bowl."

Jackson's mouth twisted a bit as he clutched those tickets in his hand like lost treasure.

"What's that look about?"

"The Super Bowl is on Sunday. I've already done my out-of-town game last week with Scottie. You know I don't like missing church like that."

"Boy, bye, you have no idea if Scottie will ever make it back to the Super Bowl. We are going to that game. Trust me, God will not forsake us because of this." Jewel started laughing at him.

"I don't see what's so funny."

"I remember a certain someone telling me that he couldn't do church because he likes to sleep in on Sundays and golf. What happened to that man?"

"I got a simulation golf course in my house. And I beat you just about every game we play."

Eyes rolling heavenward. "Really?"

Getting serious, he said, "I also grew up. And I have you to thank for that." He waved the tickets around. "So the least I can do is take you to the big game."

They got dressed and headed out of the house. Jewel strutted to the car, sing-songing, "I'm going to the Super Bowl, hey! I'm going to the Super Bowl, hey!"

They made it to church on time. Praise and worship was on high in the place this morning. Serena was leading one of his favorite worship songs, I Surrender All.

Jewel was excited to hear her sister. "That girl can sang!" She lifted her hands to the song.

Jackson was feeling it too. God was in this place, and he was so happy to be here. For once in his life, he felt fulfilled. Truly fulfilled. He'd had money before giving his life to the Lord, but he had been living in a condo all by himself, alone most of the time. Now he had a family. His family worshiped God and were better for it. "Thank You, Jesus," He said with hands lifted high.

When praise and worship ended, Pastor Walton stood behind the podium and preached a message on 'The Unprofitable Man'. He took his text from Mark 8:34-38.

[Jesus] had called the people unto him with his disciples also, he said unto them, Whosoever will come after me, let him deny himself, and take up his cross, and follow me. For whosoever will save his life shall lose it; but whosoever shall lose his life for my sake and the gospel's, the same shall save it.

For what shall it profit a man, if he shall gain the whole world, and lose his own soul? Or what shall a man give in exchange for his soul? Whosoever therefore shall be ashamed of me and of my words in this adulterous and sinful generation; of him also shall the Son of man be ashamed, when he cometh in the glory of his father with the holy angels.

Jackson's eyes fluttered open. He laid in his bed, frozen by what he'd witnessed. He usually forgot his dreams the moment he woke up. But not this one, he remembered everything, like the house he and Jewel lived in — she was going to be surprised about that for sure.

But he was surprised about the conviction he had about God. Never had he been a churchgoer, never had he wanted to be. But now...

"I can do this. I can serve God." Jackson climbed out of his bed bound and determined to no longer be an unprofitable man. He wouldn't gather the riches of this world and miss the true richness that could only come from God.

20

Butterflies danced in Jewel's stomach when she woke up. It was Sunday, and she needed to get going. But she couldn't leave the house without finding one of her most prized possessions. Although the way she'd treated it, no one would have guessed it meant anything at all to her.

"Let's see, when I moved into this apartment, I put it…"

Jewel opened the dresser drawer and searched all the way in the back of the drawer. "There it is."

Jewel thought she had no use for the dancer charm anymore. She hadn't been able to throw it away, though. So, she took it off her charm bracelet years ago, then wrapped it in plastic and tucked it away.

As she unwrapped her precious ballerina charm, so many emotions bubbled up in her that she couldn't contain them. She cried, she laughed, scratched her head as she wondered why a little piece of brass was so important that she could never throw it away, but couldn't bear to look at it.

The ballerina was dressed in pink tights and a purple leotard. It was slightly different from what Jewel had worn when she ministered in dance. But the brown skin of the charm was a constant reminder of the girl who grew up to be a woman — a woman who tried to ignore the gift God placed in her. A woman who had been too ashamed to dance. But today was a new day.

All things were possible with God, and Jewel had been invited to dance at church. All thoughts of unworthiness were gone. She would no longer hide the gift God gave her.

~~~

Heading to the airport, Jackson felt off. Like he was missing a moment that God had provided just for him. He couldn't explain it. But Jackson somehow knew that getting on the plane would be the worst mistake of his life.

Glancing at his watch, he told the cab driver, "Sorry 'bout this, but I need you to turn around."

In his African accent, the cabbie said, "If I take you back home, I'm still going to charge you for the fare."

"I'm not going back home." Jackson googled the address he needed, then gave it to the cabbie. He then made a phone call and prayed that he wasn't too late.

~~~

Standing before the congregation in pink tights and a black leotard that had once been her signature dance outfit, Jewel's eyes searched the pews for her mother. She was just three pews from the front on the right side of the pulpit, where she normally sat. "I am so sorry that I wasn't able to dance at your wedding as you wanted. I used to think that I could only minister in dance if I was the pure vessel that God wanted me to be. But it is because of God's grace that I am ready to do this again."

Jewel stretched out her arms, set her feet like a ballerina as she listened to the instrumental of *Your Will* by Darius Brooks. As the music began to play, she closed her eyes, swayed from left to right and then back again, feeling the movement of the song. Then, like a butterfly, she took flight — floating around the room, arms flailing, legs leaping, twirling, twirling, and twirling. The song ministered to her as she ministered in dance.

Her heart was breaking because she desperately wished, just like the singer, that she could tell God what she wanted out of life. But Jewel knew all too well that if it wasn't God's will for her, the thing she wanted might hurt her.

She danced out her sorrows for wanting what she couldn't have. God was being good to her by keeping her from hurt, harm, and destruction. She'd been down that road without God before. Jewel never wanted anything else in this whole world that God didn't want her to have — but it hurt.

The tempo of the song increased as the singer sung, "So, I'll cry until you tell me, let it go. Just let it be." Tears streamed down Jewel's face.

Vanetta's face was drenched in anguish as she stood and lifted her hands in praise. "It hurts Lord, it hurts, but Your will is what's best."

Jewel kept dancing, kept ministering to the people. As they felt every motion of her dance —the movement of her arms, listening to the words of the song, the congregation was overcome with emotion. They stood, waved their hands like waving a white flag, and cried out, "Your will, God. We want your will, God."

Chest heaving, tears forming a puddle around her feet, yet and still, Jewel felt God's presence, like He was saying, yes. But yes, to what?"

Then she heard Pastor Walton saying, "Didn't I say that y'all would be in for a treat today. Oh, what a mighty God we serve."

Others in the sanctuary shouted, "Praise God!"

"He is Good."

"Your will, God, is what's best for me."

Pastor Walton stood behind the pulpit, clearly enjoying the level of praise the people were sending up to the Lord. He let them continue to shout praises another minute, then lifted a hand. "God is good, oh yes He is. But I need y'all to do me a favor and have a seat."

Jewel was about to sit down as others took their seats.

"Not you, Jewel," Pastor Walton said. "Can you please come up here and stand by me at the podium?"

"Sure." Jewel glanced at her mother, wondering what Vanetta had up her sleeve. She stood next to the pastor, hands behind her back, perfect posture.

Pastor Walton started prophesying to Jewel, "That dance was a representation of your life. You poured your heart out before our very eyes. But God is saying, you don't have to cry anymore. God says that while you were preparing yourself for Him, He has been preparing someone for you."

Jewel couldn't help it. Tears sprang to her eyes. The very fact that God loved her so much that He considered even the desires of her heart amazed her.

Pastor Walton was holding Jewel's charm bracelet. He handed it to her. I was told to give this to you."

Jewel's eyes widened. Had Jackson been here? Did he watch her dance? She scanned the sanctuary. She didn't see him. But she was so thankful to have her bracelet back. She had pinned the ballerina charm to her leotard. She took it off and re-hooked it to the bracelet.

"Let me help you with that."

That was Jackson's voice. Jewel swung around. "Jackson?"

"I'm here, Jewel." He took the bracelet from her hand, put it around her arm, and clasped it.

"But I thought you had a trip this morning?"

"I cancelled it. I wanted to be in church this morning. I wanted to worship God with you, Jewel. Today and forever."

"What are you saying, Jackson?"

In answer, Jackson got on his knees. "Marry me, Jewel. Let's spend the rest of our lives together. You, me, and God. That threefold cord that will never be broken."

"Oh, my God." Her hand went to her mouth as she thought, prayer really does work.

Jackson pulled her engagement ring from his jacket pocket. He slid the ring on her finger. "I will never give you a reason to take it off again, Jewel. I'm convinced that we can do this thing. So, what do you say?"

His words were like music to her ears, a melody she could dance to. "Of course, I will marry you, Baby-Boo."

Her family ran over to them, they hugged. Bradley took Jackson to the side and said, "Welcome to the family, Son."

The Dawson and the Lewis family sat down in the sanctuary and listened as the man of God brought forth the word. There was safety in the house, and Jewel and Jackson would abide in its safety forever.

The end

Don't forget to join my mailing list:
http://vanessamiller.com/events-join-mailing-list/
Join me on Facebook: https://www.facebook.com/groups/77899021863/
Join me on Twitter: https://www.twitter.com/vanessamiller01

<u>Books in the Let's Stay Together Series</u>

Forever

Forever My Lady

Forever and a Day

Other Books by Vanessa Miller

Forever
Family Business I
Family Business II
Family Business III
Family Business IV
Family Business V
Family Business VI

Our Love
For Your Love
Got To Be Love
Rain in the Promised Land
Heaven Sent
Sunshine And Rain
After the Rain
How Sweet The Sound
Heirs of Rebellion
Feels Like Heaven
Heaven on Earth
The Best of All
Better for Us
Her Good Thing
Long Time Coming
A Promise of Forever Love
A Love for Tomorrow
Yesterday's Promise
Forgotten
Forgiven
Forsaken
Rain for Christmas (Novella)
Through the Storm
Rain Storm
Latter Rain
Abundant Rain
Former Rain

Anthologies (Editor)

Keeping the Faith
Have A Little Faith
This Far by Faith

Novella

Love Isn't Enough
A Mighty Love
The Blessed One (Blessed and Highly Favored series)
The Wild One (Blessed and Highly Favored Series)
The Preacher's Choice (Blessed and Highly Favored Series)
The Politician's Wife (Blessed and Highly Favored Series)
The Playboy's Redemption (Blessed and Highly Favored Series)
Tears Fall at Night (Praise Him Anyhow Series)
Joy Comes in the Morning (Praise Him Anyhow Series)
A Forever Kind of Love (Praise Him Anyhow Series)
Ramsey's Praise (Praise Him Anyhow Series)
Escape to Love (Praise Him Anyhow Series)
Praise For Christmas (Praise Him Anyhow Series)
His Love Walk (Praise Him Anyhow Series)
Could This Be Love (Praise Him Anyhow Series)
Song of Praise (Praise Him Anyhow Series)

Sample Chapter

Got To Be Love

Book 3

Loving You Series

By:

Vanessa Miller

Prologue

The pain was excruciating, he had never gone this far before. But the doctor confirmed that Gina had a broken arm and cracked ribs. Marvel Williams had told her that he loved her and wanted to marry her.

The nurse put a cast on her arm and then left the room as a police officer who looked like he'd just barely graduated high school stepped into the room. He was so thin, a strong wind could blow him over. Gina doubted that this man, whether police officer or not, could protect her. So, when he asked, "Who did this to you?"

She said, "I fell."

"Ma'am, your injuries aren't consistent with a fall. Tell me the truth so we can help you."

But she couldn't tell him, or something bad would happen to her, Marvel promised he'd kill her, and she believed him. He was violent and vicious. She hated him, wished him nothing but the worst. But she couldn't file a complaint because she was terrified that he would make good on his threats.

How things had turned so bad, Gina didn't know or understand. She had just received a promotion and took Marvel out to celebrate. Some guy looked at her a moment too long and everything got crazy from there. Marvel told her, "You got that promotion and now you think you can stare at other men right in my face?"

No, not again, she thought. She just wanted to enjoy an evening out with her man. She didn't want to make Marvel mad. She didn't need nor want this kind of drama in her life. "I wasn't looking at anyone. I was just sitting here talking to you."

Pushing his chair back, he stood, threw a few dollars on the table and said, "Come on, let's go."

"Please don't get upset Marvel, let's just have some fun tonight, okay?"

He grabbed her arm and snatched her out of her seat, "I said let's go."

"Are you sure you don't want to tell the police what happened," the nurse asked after the officer left the room.

Her nurse was an older woman with gray hair and kind eyes. She reminded Gina of her grandmother. She desperately wanted to tell someone about what she was going through. But she didn't see a way out, so there was no use.

"Can I pray with you?" The nurse asked.

Prayer. She'd done a lot of that as a teenager in youth ministry at her church back in Detroit, Michigan. But during college, she hadn't had much time for God or youth ministry. After college, she met Marvel, and he wasn't a churchgoer, so Gina hadn't thought much about going to church either.

Now she was in trouble and she needed God like she never needed Him before. As tears fell down her face, she said, "Please pray for me."

The nurse bowed her head as she held onto Gina's hand, the hand that didn't have the cast on it. "Lord, I come to you on behalf of this beautiful young lady. Lord, we know that You are a good God and You desire good things for us. So, I ask that you first help Gina to see the joy that comes with serving You so You can save her soul. I also ask that You lead and guide her away from all hurt, harm and danger. That includes any relationship that might be bad for her. Make a way of escape for her, Lord Jesus."

The prayer sparked a fire in Gina because it finally helped her to realize that she could escape. She just needed the Lord to show her the way.

1

Looking out the window, Gina Melson could hardly believe that the sun was shining so bright in the midwest on December 28th. It was a beautiful day for a wedding, coupled with the fact that it was still the Christmas season, so the wedding was going to be festive. Gina was excited to be a bridesmaid at her best friend's wedding. The only issue she had was that her car was not in the driveway where she left it last night. Frantic and about to call 911 to report her bright red BMW stolen, Gina then remembered the conversation she had with the bank thirty days ago.

She had been sixty days past due on the BMW at that time. They demanded their money or the key. Business had been slow, and Gina had barely been getting by. Her pantry had Ramen noodles in it, something she swore she'd never eat again after college. Her heat was even set at 68 degrees, she now had a cold and had worn out her favorite fluffy pink socks.

No matter how many adjustments she made, the money still wasn't flowing like it had when she was climbing the ladder at her old PR firm. Gina blamed Marvel Williams for all her woes. He claimed to love her, but Marvel didn't have love in his heart for anyone but himself. After breaking her arm, he belittled and terrorized her until she quit a job she loved so she could move out of the country to get away from him.

Gina used up a great deal of her savings while living in the Bahamas and basically hiding out from her abuser. When she did move back to the United States, she moved into an upscale condo division that had security. Gina was just beginning her PR firm and couldn't afford the condo, but she needed to feel safe.

Rolling her eyes at her current situation, she tried to use her cell phone to arrange an Uber pick up but the call was redirected to Sprint. Her phone had been cut off for non-payment. Gina made arrangements to pay the bill in two weeks and they reconnected her service. Where she would get that money in two weeks, Gina didn't know.

But once her phone was reconnected, she called her mom. She hadn't told her parents about her financial woes, but it couldn't be helped now. She didn't want to spend extra money on Uber when she had just made an arrangement to pay a past due cell phone bill. "I need your help, Mom."

"I'm getting ready for the wedding but let me know what I can do."

Her mom was always so accommodating, and Gina loved her for it. "I need a ride to church."

"Don't tell me that fabulous BMW of yours broke down?"

Gina hated admitting the truth but lying was not an option. She believed the words of the Bible that said a liar can't tarry in God's eyesight. So, she refused to make up lies when the truth was readily available. "I'm behind on payments so they repossessed it."

"Oh, my goodness. Do you need money?" Audrey Melson asked her daughter.

"No, Mom, I'm handling it. I just need a ride."

"Okay, hon, I'm on my way."

"Thank you." Gina hung up and waited on her mom to pick her up as if she was sixteen again, staying after school for cheerleading practice and then needed to wait on her ride to get home. Her mom picked her up and drove her to the church so she could perform her duties as a bridesmaid and that was all she really cared about right now.

Three days after Christmas, Gina would have thought that people would be off work, still enjoying the Christmas spirit and spending time with their families. But evidently, the taxman and collections departments don't close for Jesus, family, or nobody else. Gina was at her breaking point. But she had thoroughly, no-turning-back-this-time given her life to Jesus about six months ago, so she turned to Him as she sat in the passenger seat of her mother's Toyota Camry. Gina bowed her head and silently prayed, "Lord, I trust You. Things are shaking right now. I don't know what to do to get over this hump. Please help me. I need a financial breakthrough, not tomorrow or next week, but today."

"Tell Mama what's going on. How can I help you, hon?" Her mom asked while putting a hand on Gina's shoulder for comfort.

The last thing Gina wanted to do was burden her parents. They were retired and just barely getting by on the pensions they thought would carry them through. "It will be alright, Mom. Being my chauffeur is a tremendous help to me. And you drive around listening to praise music. What?" Gina turned up the radio and started rocking to *Can't Nobody Do Me Like Jesus* by Maranatha Gospel.

Popping her fingers and steady rocking, Gina said, "What that man say, Mama?"

"I hear him… can't nobody do you like Jesus, so you want your Mama to step back." Audrey nodded, understanding her limitations now that her daughter was a full-grown woman.

Gina exhaled as they pulled up to Christ-Life Sanctuary. She was truly enjoying the praise music and it was encouraging her soul. But in truth, she'd only turned up the volume to get her mother to think about Jesus rather than her daughter's problems.

They got out of the car and Gina's mother looped her arm around her arm. "Trouble don't last always," Audrey said to Gina as they entered the church.

Before the weariness she was feeling could set in, Gina activated her faith and pointed heavenward." It can't last forever, because we belong to Him."

Audrey brought Gina's head to her shoulder as she laid a kiss on her forehead. "I'm so thankful to God that you came back home."

"Me too, Mama." She left her mother in the entryway and went to the back of the church, where the bridal party was using the prayer room to get dressed.

"You made it." Toya Milner opened her arms for a hug as she sat at the table, having lash extensions added to her eyelashes.

Gina rushed to her best friend and hugged her. "Of course, I made it. I wouldn't miss your big day for anything."

"Help!" Toya called out.

"What's wrong?" Gina stepped back. "Was I hugging you too tight?"

"I can't open my eyes."

The best laugh she'd had all week occurred while watching Toya try to open her eyes as the glue from the eyelash extensions on the top eyelid connected with the bottom lid and stuck together.

Toya's eyelashes fluttered; the glue still wouldn't give. Then the make-up artist started flaring her arms like she was coming in for a landing, "I told you not to blink. Didn't I tell you?"

"How can I avoid blinking? Eyes blink. That's what they do." Toya kept struggling to open her eyes.

The make-up artist worked on the lashes, trying to pull them apart and Gina grabbed her belly as she doubled over laughing. "I'm sorry, I'm sorry. I know this shouldn't be so funny to me, but I need this laugh today."

"And I need my eyes to stay open so I can walk down the aisle and marry my man." Toya widened her eyes, trying to keep the lashes from touching again.

Gina wanted to stop laughing but Toya looked so silly while holding her eyes open like that. The make-up artist didn't help the situation as she stood in front of Toya with a mini fan on high. Blowing hot breath in Toya's face. "Men will never understand what we women go through to be beautiful and glamorous."

"Tia, Toya's younger sister agreed. "And all they have to do is shave and throw on their clothes, then stand there complaining about how slow we are."

Gina then told Toya, "Next time get the strip lashes. Those individual lashes are more pain than they are worth."

"Tia talked me into it." Toya pointed toward her very pregnant sister.

"Don't blame me." Tia held onto her stomach as she struggled to stand and waddle over to her sister. "I can't be held responsible for anything I say or do until this baby comes out."

"How much longer," Gina asked.

"Three more weeks."

"Looks like you ready to pop today. Don't let your water break and get all over my shoes while we're standing at the altar." Gina glanced down at her gray Manolo Blahnik's. They were the most expensive pair of shoes she owned other than a pair of glittery Jimmy Choo's that she normally brought out on New Year's Eve. But she would probably be selling her precious shoes at a second time around shop if things didn't turn around quickly. Probably should have gotten rid of them a long time ago anyway since they had been gifts from her evil ex. But most women would have agreed with her decision… get rid of the man, keep the shoes.

~~~

To continue reading click the link below:

https://www.amazon.com/Got-Love-Loving-You-Book-ebook/dp/B082KKJXZY/ref=sr_1_1?crid=32O8OMDLYIDF2&dchild=1&keywords=got+to+be+love+vanessa+miller&qid=1597896486&s=books&sprefix=Got+To+Be+Love+Vanessa+Miller%2Cstripbooks%2C181&sr=1-1

About the Author

Vanessa Miller is a best-selling author, entrepreneur, playwright, and motivational speaker. She started writing as a child, spending countless hours either reading or writing poetry, short stories, stage plays and novels. Vanessa's creative endeavors took on new meaning in1994 when she became a Christian. Since then, her writing has been centered on themes of redemption, often focusing on characters facing multi-dimensional struggles.

Vanessa's novels have received rave reviews, with several appearing on *Essence Magazine's* Bestseller's List. Miller's work has receiving numerous awards, including "Best Christian Fiction Mahogany Award" and the "Red Rose Award for Excellence in Christian Fiction." Miller graduated from Capital University with a degree in Organizational Communication. She is an ordained minister in her church, explaining, "God has called me to minister to readers and to help them rediscover their place with the Lord."

She has worked with numerous publishers: Urban Christian, Kimani Romance, Abingdon Press and Whitaker House. She is currently working on the Let's Stay Together series.

In 2016, Vanessa launched the Christian Book Lover's Retreat in an effort to bring readers and authors of Christian fiction together in an environment that's all about Faith, Fun & Fellowship. To learn more about Vanessa, please visit her website: www.vanessamiller.com. If you would like to know more about the Christian Book Lover's

Retreat that is currently held in Charlotte, NC during the last week in October you can visit:

http://www.christianbookloversretreat.com/index.html

Don't forget to join my mailing list:
http://vanessamiller.com/events/join-mailing-list/
Join me on Facebook: **https://www.facebook.com/groups/77899021863/**
Join me on Twitter: **https://www.twitter.com/vanessamiller01**

Made in the USA
Columbia, SC
01 September 2020